The Eleventh Armada Ghost Book

D1425181

This Armada book belongs to:

Donna Davies,
Sherrogh, Sinclare
bare, Halkirk.

Other Spinechillers in Armada

Armada Ghost Books Nos. 1-10
edited by Christine Bernard and Mary Danby

Armada Monster Books Nos. 1-5
edited by R. Chetwynd-Hayes

A Shiver of Spooks
edited by Christine Bernard

Armada Sci-Fi 1-4
edited by Richard Davis

The Monster Trap and Other True Mysteries
The Restless Bones and Other True Mysteries
by Peter Haining

Fun to Know About Ghosts
by Sean Richards

The Eleventh Armada Ghost Book

Edited by Mary Danby

Illustrated by Peter Archer

The Eleventh Armada Ghost Book was first
published in the U.K. in 1979 by
Fontana Paperbacks,
14 St. James's Place, London SW1A 1PS

The arrangement of this collection is copyright
© Mary Danby 1979

Printed in Great Britain by Love & Malcomson Ltd.,
Brighton Road, Redhill, Surrey.

CONDITIONS OF SALE:
This book is sold subject to the condition that
it shall not, by way of trade or otherwise, be lent,
re-sold, hired out or otherwise circulated without
the publisher's prior consent in any form of
binding or cover other than that in which it is
published and without a similar condition
including this condition being imposed on the
subsequent purchaser.

CONTENTS

INTRODUCTION 7

THE GREEN GHOST 9
Terry Tapp

THE KING STONE 24
Margaret Biggs

TOM 35
Frank Richards

THE LAVENDER LADY 45
Valerie Waters

MAGIC ON THE FIELD 52
Eve Gothard

STELLA 66
Rosemary Timperley

THIS BOOK BELONGS TO . . . 74
Daphne Froome

A GHOST IN THE FAMILY 83
Christine Pullein-Thompson

THE GHOSTLY GARDENERS 94
Ruth Cameron

THE OLD SIEGE HOUSE 106
Sydney J. Bounds

THE HOUSE GHOSTS 114
Mary Danby

ACKNOWLEDGEMENTS

The editor gratefully acknowledges permission to reprint copyright material to the following:

Terry Tapp for THE GREEN GHOST. © Terry Tapp 1979.

Margaret Biggs for THE KING STONE. © Margaret Biggs 1979.

Frank Richards for TOM. © Frank Richards 1979.

Valerie Waters for THE LAVENDER LADY. © Valerie Waters 1979.

Eve Gothard for MAGIC ON THE FIELD. © Eve Gothard 1979.

Rosemary Timperley and Harvey Unna & Stephen Durbridge Ltd. for STELLA. © Rosemary Timperley 1979.

Daphne Froome for THIS BOOK BELONGS TO . . . © Daphne Froome 1979.

Christine Pullein-Thompson for A GHOST IN THE FAMILY. © Christine Pullein-Thompson 1979.

Ruth Cameron and Harvey Unna & Stephen Durbridge Ltd. for THE GHOSTLY GARDENERS. © Ruth Cameron 1979.

Sydney J. Bounds for THE OLD SIEGE HOUSE. © Sydney J. Bounds 1979.

THE HOUSE GHOSTS is © Mary Danby 1979.

INTRODUCTION

THE eleventh Armada Ghost Book—and eleven new stories of spectral delight.

Most people like to scare themselves a little—so long as the ghosts stick to the printed page and don't wander abroad. But though it's fun to read about a ghost, imagine meeting one face to face (or face to skull, perhaps). That might be quite another story! Anyway, you won't need to read these stories in a moonlit churchyard—they have quite enough built-in spookiness of their own.

In *The Green Ghost*, you can meet a truly terrifying apparition. Mind you, it seems that Emma's friend Thumb-sucker is more than a match for him, which is just as well . . .

The King Stone stands majestically on a Scottish island, and Ross is horrifyingly drawn into the evil that surrounds it, while Jane Carter faces terror of another kind in *Tom* —the story of a great black dog with eyes like fire . . .

A very sad ghost haunts Lavender Cottage, and Simon and Debbie are determined to solve the weird and frightening mystery of *The Lavender Lady*. Next comes football-mad Gerry. With Phil's help, he might make the school team, but Phil is such a strange, silent boy. Still, he's *Magic on the Field* . . .

In *Stella*, an Underground train journey leads to a very peculiar and wonderful destination—the end of the line, in fact. But Robert comes back . . . Jenny, too, has a strange experience. Why is she haunted by the ghost of a young Victorian girl? Read *This Book Belongs To* . . . and you'll know the answer.

Wouldn't it be nice to have a ghostly ancestor? Or would it? In *A Ghost in the Family*, it turns out to be not so much fun after all. In *The Ghostly Gardeners*, however,

7

the phantoms are definitely of the friendly variety, and an ill boy has cause to be thankful he found them.

The Old Siege House, built on the site of an old castle, holds many a secret. "Bring out your ghosts!" shouts Alf, and it does—to teach him a lesson he'll never forget.

The House Ghosts are Albert and Victoria, a somewhat elderly pair of spectral beings. They have been forbidden to haunt, but when it comes to getting rid of an unwelcome guest, they turn out to be decidedly young in spirit. Perhaps you have house ghosts. Ask someone like Aunt Prudence to stay, and you may find out . . .

Have a deliciously eerie read!

MARY DANBY

THE GREEN GHOST

by Terry Tapp

OF one thing Emma Finch was absolutely certain: there is a life after death. She knew this as surely as she knew that night followed day, and she was quietly happy with her knowledge. Furthermore, Emma believed in ghosts. She believed in good ghosts and bad ghosts, and she most certainly believed in the Green Ghost that haunted Brampton Hall. What Emma did not know—and she intended to rectify that within the next few minutes—was whether Brampton Hall was *still* haunted by the Green Ghost of her childhood memories. After all, a lot can happen in eighty years.

Trudging up the steep, gravel drive to Brampton Hall, Emma was pleasantly surprised to note that the immense Victorian house had lost much of its bleak, forbidding appearance over the years. The bright blue curtains at each window were such a contrast to the deep brown curtains of her own era. And the garden was friendly too; a child's swing, a bicycle and a brightly coloured beach ball persuaded her that Brampton Hall was now a happy family home.

Now Emma stood before the massive oak door of Brampton Hall, her jaw set resolutely as she gripped the lion-head doorknocker and clamped it hard against the iron spike. Still holding the doorknocker, reluctant to let go of it, her mind spanned the years back to the time when people came to Brampton Hall on horseback, or in fine coaches. How many hands, she wondered, have gripped this very doorknocker?

Emma was about to knock again when she noticed a

new bell-push set into the door jamb; she pressed it once. The resulting pandemonium caused her to jump back from the door in alarm. Two gigantic, hairy, barking, bounding, rollicking, shapeless dogs skidded joyfully around the house to greet her.

"Oh!" Emma cried. "Down, boys. You'll get my coat dirty."

She pressed the bell again, twice this time, her eyes fixed on the dogs as they barked and scampered around her, darting in at her legs, then turning away at the very last moment.

With some relief she heard the door bolt slide back and she smiled at the little girl who stood there, thumb in mouth, a scowl upon her pretty young face.

"Hello," said Emma. "Is your daddy or mummy at home?"

The child stared vacantly at her.

"Well?" Emma gave the girl an encouraging smile. "Are they?"

The child considered the question awhile, appeared to make some decision, and slammed the door hard in Emma's face, causing the two dogs, who had been watching events with pricked ears, to jump to their feet and set up a terrible row. After what seemed like a lifetime all over again, the door opened and the girl reappeared, thumb still wedged in her mouth.

"Yes," she said. "Mummy is here."

"I wonder if I might have a word with her."

Thumbsucker considered that question, too, as if everything Emma said demanded the utmost thought. Suddenly, without warning, she removed her thumb from her mouth and shouted at the top of her voice: "Mummy! There's an old lady here and she wants to talk to you!"

"An old lady?" That was a boy's voice.

"What—a witch?" A younger boy shouted that.

"No," said Thumbsucker. "She isn't a witch. She's just very, very old."

By now the two boys had clattered down the stairs and

were standing before Emma, inspecting her with the unashamed curiosity children sometimes display.

"What does she want?" asked the smaller boy.

"Dunno," said Thumbsucker.

Then the dogs started barking again, bored with listening to human conversation. The two boys let out earpiercing whoops and shot from the doorway like arrows, chasing the delighted dogs back around the house where they had come from.

As Emma turned back to face Thumbsucker, she saw a young woman hurrying towards the door, wiping her hands on her apron.

"What is it?" she asked.

"This old woman," said Thumbsucker. "She wants you for something."

"Really!" The child's mother made an exasperated face. Then smiled at Emma. "Sorry to have kept you waiting—I didn't know if there was really someone at the door, or if she was playing a trick."

"Lovely children," Emma said.

"Lovely, *rude* children," was the reply. "I do apologise for their bad manners."

"Please, don't apologise," said Emma. "They are right, you know—I *am* an old lady. Sometimes I have to be reminded of the fact."

They both laughed at that, and then Emma explained the reason for her visit. "I would, very much, like to look over Brampton Hall again."

"Again?"

"Yes, I used to live here."

"Oh, really?"

"My entire childhood was spent in this very house, and it would be nice to view it."

The young woman looked puzzled. "View? Brampton Hall is not for sale, you know."

"I realise that," Emma said. "Anyway, I couldn't afford it even if it *was* for sale. What would I do with a large place like this to keep up?"

"Well, perhaps you had better come inside," said the woman. "My name is Jean Williams, by the way."

"I'm Miss Finch," Emma said. "Miss Emma Finch."

She stepped into the hallway and stared around her. The place had hardly changed at all over the years; it was uncanny. She breathed in the rich, lingering woody smell as she surveyed the carved wall panels. Suddenly, she was a child again, as she relived the memories so vividly. She could hear the laughter and the household noises of her childhood as plainly as if they were happening that very moment. Games of tag along the corridors, the sweet, enticing aroma of spiced cooking. It was all returning, unharmed by the voyage of years. Now she could see the rosy-faced cook, wide-eyed and smiling with pride as she carried the platter of Christmas meats, the pert faces of the two young housemaids watching the proceedings, yet struggling to keep hidden. Emma had adored the maids.

Now there was the smell of apples and woodsmoke, evoking autumn and shortening days. When Emma looked at the parlour door, she could almost hear the low, grumbling conversation of her father. What a serious man he was.

"Miss Finch?"

Emma looked at the young woman in mild surprise.

"You may have a look around if you wish," said Mrs. Williams with a smile. "I've been talking to you—but you were miles away."

"Was I?" Then Emma realised that she had been so absorbed in her memories, she had lost track of the present. "Yes, I suppose I was. It really is quite an exhilarating experience returning to Brampton Hall. I had such a happy childhood here."

Mrs. Williams smiled. "Is this the first time you have seen Brampton Hall since your childhood?"

"The first time I have been inside," said Emma. "I have, on many occasions, passed by and glanced up the driveway, not daring to knock at the door."

"Well, you feel free to walk around as you please. You

must forgive the children's bedrooms. I have told them that they must keep their own rooms tidy and, I'm afraid, they aren't very good at it yet. I'm determined to let the rooms go until they learn their lesson."

"I'm sorry if I have called at an inconvenient time," Emma said.

"It's no trouble."

"You are very kind."

"If you will excuse me, then . . ." said Mrs. Williams, making for the stairs. "I really do have a lot of work to get through." Emma nodded absently, already absorbed in memories.

"I'll be in the kitchen," Mrs. Williams told her. "And if the children start to make nuisances of themselves, send them to me."

"I will," Emma promised. "Thank you."

Standing on the bottom tread of the wide, twisting staircase, Emma looked up at the stained-glass windows, recalling how, on a bright summer day, the sun would tumble through the coloured glass and light up the whole hall like a carnival. She smiled, happy that the memories had not faded with the years; in fact, if anything, the memories had been enhanced by the passing of time. Once again she placed her gloved hand on the polished balustrade and then, on impulse, removed the glove so that she could feel the hard, enduring wood.

Slowly, savouring every step like a fine meal, Emma walked up the staircase, memories flooding in on her so fast that she had, at times, to stop and wait until the kaleidoscope of faces and events had settled in her mind. Each step disturbed the dusts of forgetfulness, and she was amazed at the things which she was able to remember, amazed and delighted.

There had been no major structural changes in the old house, and Emma was able to locate the rooms confidently. She turned at the top of the stairs, walked along to the far end of the narrow corridor which led to the servants' annexe and decided to explore the east wing

13

first. The door of the master bedroom was ajar. Emma tapped gently, waited for a reply and, when there was none, she stepped into the room, her heart pounding against her ribs.

Full circle, Emma thought. Return to the birthplace.

The room was bathed in mellow, yellow sunlight which splashed the walls and furniture like butter. It was, Emma considered, miraculous how little the room had changed in appearance. The Italian marble fireplace still looked new, and the ornate ceiling was as perfect now as it was in her memory. Apart from the addition of some rather bright wallpaper and several pictures, the room was timeless and unchanged.

"What are you looking for?"

Emma wheeled around, startled at the unexpected intrusion of the child's voice. Thumbsucker was standing in the doorway, her thumb still lodged in her mouth.

"I'm not looking *for* anything," said Emma. "I'm looking *at* things."

"What are you looking at?"

"Everything," Emma replied. "I just want to look at everything and remember how the house used to be. You know, apart from the fact that we had oil lighting, then gaslight, the house is much the same as when I was your age."

"Gaslight?"

"Yes," said Emma. "We used to have a centre light in this room and wall brackets over there." She indicated the far wall.

"Do you want to see my room?" Thumbsucker asked.

Emma smiled at her; she was a pretty child, about seven years old, with small, rather pert features.

"I would love to see your room," she said. "Lead the way."

The little girl removed her thumb from her mouth and offered her hand to Emma, who pretended not to notice; she certainly did not want to hold that sticky, wet little hand. From the master bedroom, they went out to the

14

corridor, along the landing above the stairs until they reached the four smaller bedrooms. "This is mine," said Thumbsucker, kicking the door open with her foot.

"How lovely!" Emma cried, thinking exactly the opposite. The room was a jumble of toys, books, dolls and clothes. "My, this is a bright little room." She had to tread most carefully in order to avoid treading on the toys which were strewn across the floor.

"I fink it's awful," Thumbsucker said. "Mummy says she won't tidy it up for me."

"Quite right, too."

"But it's in such a mess."

"And who made it into such a mess?" Emma asked, trying to keep a straight face.

"It jus' happened," Thumbsucker replied. "Do you like my wallpaper?"

Following the young girl's gaze, Emma surveyed the psychedelic paper which covered the chimney breast. It was a brightly coloured paper, screaming, sickening, gaudy and busy-looking. "It is very—unusual," Emma said, feeling almost giddy as she groped for the edge of the bed. "Yes, very unusual indeed."

"Robin chose it for himself," Thumbsucker said. "He got Daddy to buy the paper."

"Did Robin used to sleep here?"

"Only for a while," said Thumbsucker. "Then he got scared, and I had to sleep here."

"Scared?"

Thumbsucker nodded vigorously.

"What was he scared of?"

"Ghosts," the child replied. "Robin is scared of ghosts."

"And he thought there were ghosts in this room?"

"There *was* a ghost here," Thumbsucker said. "Robin saw it and he cried."

"Have you seen it?" Emma asked, trying to keep her voice as calm as possible.

"I saw it—once."

"Were you frightened?" Now Emma was excited. Was

15

it possible that Thumbsucker had seen the ghost of her childhood? It was very important to Emma to know the answer. But the child was engrossed in rummaging through her toys, apparently having lost all interest in the conversation. Determined to get an answer, Emma reached down and lifted the child on to her lap.

"You went a funny colour when you lifted me," Thumbsucker observed seriously.

"I expect I did," Emma said, "Sometimes I forget myself and do things which I ought not to do."

"So do I," Thumbsucker said confidently. "Yesterday I made a cake in the kitchen and Mummy told me off for making a mess."

"How long ago did you see the ghost?" Emma asked.

"Last year."

"I would be most interested to hear all about it," Emma said, trying very hard to conceal her impatience. "Would you like to tell me the story, starting from the very beginning?"

Thumbsucker gazed up at the ceiling as if searching for inspiration, her face creased in concentration. Sucking hard on her thumb, the girl started to speak. Emma gently took her wrist and pulled the thumb from the girl's mouth so she could hear what she was saying.

"You got bony knees," Thumbsucker told her, with the candid truthfulness of the very young.

"Yes, I know," Emma said. "But you must tell me about the ghost. It is very important to me."

"Well, it all started when Robin asked Daddy for this wallpaper," Thumbsucker said. Emma listened as the child related the tale, interrupting now and then to make quite sure that she had heard correctly, for Thumbsucker kept pushing her thumb back into her mouth out of habit.

It seemed that Robin had set his heart on the bedroom as soon as they had moved in, because he wanted to make it into his private den. Against his own better judgement, Mr. Williams had promised Robin that he might choose his own decorations, and the result of that had been the psychedelic wallpaper. But, within a few days of moving into the room, Robin had started to complain of funny noises and voices which kept him awake at nights.

"The room is haunted," Robin had told his father.

Mr. Williams would not hear of such a thing. "Nonsense," he had told Robin sternly. "There are no such things as ghosts."

Thumbsucker had, of course, been enchanted by tales of hauntings and she had begged Robin to exchange rooms with her.

"But didn't the thought of seeing a ghost frighten you?" Emma asked.

"I *wanted* to see him," said Thumbsucker.

"So you exchanged rooms with Robin. What happened next?"

Thumbsucker began to tell the story of her first night in the room, and Emma listened eagerly, remembering the nights that she had spent in that very room. It was uncanny how very similar the stories were.

"After I had kissed Mummy goodnight, I tried to go to sleep right away," said Thumbsucker, her face rumpled with deep frowns as she concentrated. "It was hard getting to sleep in a new room, and I kept waking up because there were funny noises going on. I had to sleep in Robin's old bed and it's got all lumps in it and his pillow is harder than mine. I stayed awake for hours. I even heard Daddy and Mummy come up to bed."

"My!" said Emma. "That must have been very late indeed."

"It was," said Thumbsucker. "Anyway, that's when the green smoke came."

"Green smoke?" Emma asked, her voice trembling with excitement.

"Yes, green smoke. I was looking over at Bunnylite when I suddenly saw green smoke drifting up from my bed."

"Good gracious!" Emma said. "What did you do?"

"I was frightened at first. I thought my bed was on fire.

17

Then the smoke sort of hung in the air and I could see a green light in the very centre of it."

"Luminous," said Emma.

"The green light got brighter and brighter, lighting up the room until it was brighter than Bunnylite. Through the mistiness, I thought I could see a face. Then, after a while, the face became clearer and I could see that it was an old, old man. He was even older than you."

"Then he must have been very ancient," Emma said without a trace of a smile.

"The old man had a green face and it was covered with warts," Thumbsucker said, her eyes wide open as she recalled the horrible apparition. "He was screaming at me, his eyes alight like fire."

"The Green Ghost of Brampton Hall," Emma whispered, but Thumbsucker was too immersed in her story to hear.

"It was cold, even in my bed, and I could see that the ghost was coming for me. I wanted to hide my head under the bedclothes, but I was too scared. He laughed, showing all his bad teeth, and when his mouth was opened wide I could see that, instead of a tongue, he had a snake!"

"A snake?" cried Emma, holding Thumbsucker close for comfort as if she were a doll. How many times had she seen that precise nightmarish face?

"It was a snake, coiling in the ghost's mouth, hissing at me. The ghost came nearer until his face was almost touching mine and then he opened his mouth again and the snake slid out, over his chin, and dangled in front of my face. I cried."

"I know," said Emma, rocking the child. "I know. It is a truly dreadful thing to see."

"Then he started to grow bigger, laughing all the time. It was as if he had taken a deep breath and his whole body swelled up. He filled up the room with his body and his laughing. His hands were near my face, and his fingers were long and knobbly, with nails like claws. The nails were bright red."

18

"I thought I could see a face . . ."

19

But Emma wasn't even listening now; she had become absorbed in her own memories of the evil ghost. She, too, felt the chill and the dank, cold clamminess as she recalled those terrible nights when the Green Ghost had haunted Brampton Hall.

"Then his talons touched my face," Emma said, completely oblivious of the fact that she had interrupted Thumbsucker. "His talons bore down on me, burning and scratching. And his eyes! They were bright, like emeralds, and so very, very evil." Emma was living her childhood again. She could see the malevolent, fluorescent face as it leered at her; she could feel those burning claws and smell the cold, dank smell of decaying food. "So he is still here," she said, realising that she was frightening Thumbsucker.

"No."

"What do you mean?"

"He frightened me, so I sent him packing."

"How did you manage to do that?"

"Well, I thought it was very clever the way he kept changing shape, but I didn't like the funder."

"Funder?"

"Yes, it was loud funder and there wasn't any lightning."

"Ah—thunder," Emma said.

"It was very loud—much louder than his laughing. The noise was making my room shake, and I got scared in case Daddy thought it was me making all the noise. I get blamed for everything around here."

Emma smiled. "Do you, indeed?"

"That's when I told him to buzz off."

"You told the Green Ghost of Brampton Hall to buzz off?"

"Yes," said Thumbsucker. "I told him that he was making too much noise. So he went."

"What? You mean he just disappeared?"

"He sort of melted," said Thumbsucker thoughtfully. "It was like butter on toast. His green face seemed to melt and the smoke became thinner until he was all gone."

"How very brave of you," Emma said.

"I still don't understand why he just went when I told him to."

"You probably shamed him into it," said Emma. "Hurt his professional pride, no doubt. Nothing could be more demoralising for a ghost than to be told to buzz off. Now, think very, very carefully. Have you ever seen him since?"

"No. He hasn't been back."

"How about other ghosts?"

"Other ghosts?"

"Yes. Have you ever seen a different ghost to the Green Ghost of Brampton Hall?"

"No," Thumbsucker said. "Do you think there will be one?"

"I shouldn't be surprised at all," Emma said. "Usually a house is visited by just one ghost, but if he disappears another ghost may sometimes take his place."

"I haven't seen one," Thumbsucker said.

"You are sure?"

"Yes. I would know if I had."

"Of course you would," said Emma. "Of course."

She got up from the bed, a smile upon her face, her eyes alight with happiness. "So the Green Ghost has gone at last."

"Come on," said Thumbsucker. "I'll show you the rest of the house. Would you like to see Robin's room?"

"Yes, that would be nice."

"After that we can see Philip's room, and then I can show you Daddy's study."

Emma followed the child, drinking in the memories as she entered each room. Everything—everything that mattered—was substantially the same. The house was still alive with people, and the bricks and slates were still there. The floors were the same floors which she, as a child, had scampered across. Even the fifth stair from the top still creaked loudly when it was trodden on. Somehow Emma had the feeling that Brampton Hall was indestructible;

built before she was born, it would still be there, strong and immovable, long after she was dead and forgotten. It was a monument, in brick and stone, to Emma's happy childhood. Yes, Brampton Hall would endure to see many generations come and go.

It was a satisfying thought.

"I hope she isn't bothering you," said Mrs. Williams, appearing suddenly at the foot of the stairs. "I could hear her chattering away all the time."

"On the contrary," said Emma. "We have had a most interesting discussion."

"And I haven't been naughty," Thumbsucker added.

Emma started down the stairs, smiling as her foot touched the fifth one from the top. "You have been most kind to allow me this visit. I have enjoyed it so much."

"You are welcome," Mrs. Williams replied. "Now you must come into the kitchen and have a cup of tea. I've just made a fresh pot."

So they went into the big, warm kitchen, and Emma was delighted to see that the old kitchen range was still in use, sparkling as brightly as ever it did when she was young. The thick, crackling logs burned red and cosy, sending busy flames up to the massive iron kettle which sang and sighed in ecstasy. The whole house breathed contentment.

"Well?" asked Mrs. Williams. "Do you still like your old home?"

"I love it," Emma said fervently. "It will do very nicely indeed, I am sure of that."

"Do?" asked Mrs. Williams.

"Oh, yes. Very nicely indeed," Emma replied absently. "Especially now that the Green Ghost is gone."

"Green Ghost? Ah, you've been listening to make-believe stories," said Mrs. Williams as she poured out a cup of tea and offered Emma a plate of home-made cakes.

They talked for nearly an hour, Emma delighting Mrs. Williams with her reminiscences. When it was time for Emma to leave, she insisted on giving Thumbsucker fifty pence for telling her about the Green Ghost. "I am so glad he has gone," she said.

"Please come again," Mrs. Williams said as she saw Emma to the door. "I enjoyed hearing about Brampton Hall as it was all those years ago."

"I will," Emma promised. "I'd love to come again."

But Emma never did return to Brampton Hall to delight Mrs. Williams with more stories of her childhood. She waved goodbye and trudged back down the crunchy gravel drive, her heart beating excitedly. She smiled, turned and waved and was gone.

Some months later, as Thumbsucker lay upon her bed, in the throes of sticking Christmas cards into her scrap book, Emma came to her and sat on the edge of the bed.

"Where did you come from?" asked Thumbsucker.

"I just came," Emma said happily.

"Do you want to see around the house again?"

"No, thank you," Emma replied. "I've come to stay, this time. I'm going to stay here for ever and ever."

"Until you die?" asked Thumbsucker.

"Until I get told to buzz off," Emma replied with a twinkle in her eye.

"I wouldn't ever tell you to buzz off," Thumbsucker said. "I like having you here."

"That is nice to hear," Emma replied. "I'll try very hard not to make a nuisance of myself." Then she rose from the bed, crossed the room and floated straight through the bedroom door.

THE KING STONE

by MARGARET BIGGS

"OH look, Ross, there it is!" cried Meg, grabbing my arm as we leant on the steamer rail.

Suddenly the thick sea-mist was lifting, and the boat was near enough to the Isle of Arran for us to see Goat Fell starkly uprising against the windy grey sky. Immediately I felt an odd pang, a thrill of fear and bewildering recognition.

"Doesn't it look wild, Ross," Meg said, while the wind tore at our hair and the gulls hovered, screaming, overhead. She shivered and pulled her anorak tighter round her. "Look at all the mountains with the mist around them!" She paused. "Do you think we'll like it here?"

"Don't worry, it'll be all right," I said, acting bored.

We were going to stay on a farm on the island for a fortnight. Meg had been ill, and Mum couldn't get away from her job, so I was in charge. I didn't mind—I was fond of Meg and used to bossing her and keeping an eye on her. I was three years older than her, and fourteen is pretty adult, after all, as I told Mum when she fussed a bit.

Now the steamer was cutting swiftly through the grey-blue water, leaving a line of creamy foam to disappear in our wake. Brodick harbour was coming closer, and we would soon be there. The boat's hooter wailed, people on the quayside moved forward, and in a few minutes we were tying up and unloading. I gazed at the clustered houses. No, I had never seen *them* before—yet the bleak heights of Goat Fell looming above us made me unaccountably tense and on edge. It was strange, because Meg was usually the one whose imagination took wing, and I usually the one who brought her back to earth.

24

I glanced at our map. Beside Goat Fell lay more curves and heads—the Sleeping Warrior, according to the map, and undoubtedly shaped like a stretched-out recumbent figure. My eyes lingered on the hills. Brodick village looked a peaceful, tranquil little place—but those hills towering above were utterly different, timeless and menacing.

We clattered down the gangway, swinging our bags. There was a salty tang in the air, a sense of freedom and emptiness. It was another world from the Midlands, which we had left early that morning. Our family was Scottish, but we had never been over the border before.

"Mum said Mr. McLellan would meet the boat," Meg breathlessly reminded me, at my heels.

"That's probably him, waving," I answered, seeing a brown-faced, burly man leaning against the bonnet of an ancient car.

"So here you are! Give me those bags."

A couple of minutes later we were out of the village and driving along the String, the road that cut in curves through the centre of the island. Mr. McLellan bumped us along, sometimes waving a brown arm at one of the hills as he called out a Gaelic name. The hills reared up on either side of the steeply rising mountain road. We saw sheep, who lifted their heads to stare at us as we passed, but no red deer—they were higher up, and the mist was hiding them, Mr. McLellan told us. There were plenty of them, and a fine nuisance to the crops they were every spring! It was all very well for visitors to rave about them, but they'd broken his fences many a time.

After a few miles we swung off the String on to a smaller, rougher lane, which bounced us gradually back down to sea level. Now we could see the sea surrounding us on three sides. To the other lay open moorland, pale green with darker green bracken and boggy patches, and long grass straining in the keen wind, and an air of utter remoteness. Invisible above us, birds were calling in high-pitched wails—curlews, Mr. McLellan told us. "Yon's Machrie Moor," he added laconically.

Looking at it I felt again, more strongly, that strange stab of remembrance mixed with fear. I gazed at the moor, expecting, yet dreading, to see something. Why on earth should this lonely place summon up such feelings? I was angry with myself. It was stupid. Had I seen a picture of the moor somewhere, and forgotten it?

Down, down the lane, and on nearer the sea, and then at last a twisty turn up a stony path, and we jerked into the lonely croft where the McLellans lived, and Mrs. McLellan took visitors sometimes. A friend had given Mum her address, and said it was just the spot for Meg to get strong again after scarlet fever. We got out stiffly, and the wind whipped at our hair. The moor lay close all around the small low croft. The gulls swooped and cried over our heads. It was the edge of the world.

"I love it, don't you?" Meg said in my ear, her blue eyes glowing.

I nodded—but my feelings were hopelessly mixed, and I couldn't untangle them. It was beautiful—but threatening.

Mrs. McLellan came out, small and plump and smiling, wreathed in an old-fashioned apron. She said tea was all ready, with fresh eggs and cream and jam on fresh-baked scones, and would we like to take our cases upstairs? Up the few narrow stairs we went, and I ducked my head just in time to miss a wooden beam. There were two tiny rooms up there, side by side.

"Can I have this one, Ross? It looks out on the sea," Meg said eagerly, her face looking pinker and less drawn already. She always loved the sea.

"All right, I don't mind. This one's just as good." I went into the other little room, ducking my head again under the lintel. The whitewashed ceiling was bumpy and low. I dumped my case and went over to the window. The casement stood open, the faded curtains flapped. I leaned out, and a shudder shook my whole body. Beyond, on the moor, perhaps two hundred yards away, stood an incomplete circle of dark grey, weathered, standing stones.

Danger—danger! screamed a voice in my head. Hide! Angrily I stared at the stones. They drew and held my gaze irresistibly. Silent, motionless, brooding, like untiring watchers they stood waiting—waiting for what? My eyes settled uneasily on the tallest, a head taller than the others. It faced the croft squarely, leaning forward, its shape like humped shoulders. I scowled at it, fighting down a sick, queasy feeling.

I had seen the stones before. I knew too well the shape of each one, but the tallest was the one I dreaded most of all, the one I had to drag my eyes away from.

I said nothing to Meg, of course, and over tea we got chatting to the McLellans, and I tried to concentrate on what they were saying. Their children had grown up and gone away to live on the mainland, Mrs. McLellan told us, but she and her husband would never leave. They had been born here, and the island was in their blood. Their eldest son wanted them to sell up and go to Glasgow with him—but no, they would stay where they were. Machrie was the place for them. The loneliness never troubled them.

We were tired after our long journey, too tired to explore that night. It was still light when we went yawning up to bed. We were so far west, Mr. McLellan told us, it was light until midnight at midsummer. Even now, in the spring, it was light till almost eleven. That seemed uncanny. In my pyjamas I drew back the curtains before getting into bed. There were the stones, silhouetted and watching against the darkening sky. I stared at them for a long moment, and I was uncomfortably aware of their power. Hastily I snatched the curtains across again. I didn't want to see them—and I didn't want them to see me.

I fell asleep quickly in Mrs. McLellan's thyme-scented, darned sheets. Soon I began to dream. I dreamt of the stones. They were calling to me, lumbering heavily towards me, encircling me so that I couldn't escape. They grew larger and larger, crowding and jostling round me. Then one of them spoke, and I knew which one it was.

"Come, you must come. I am waiting for you. I have waited a long time," he said slowly.

At these words I woke up with a violent jerk. My face was sweaty, and my hands. I found I was clutching the pillow tightly. I lay hearing my heart thump, and tried to calm down. Meg sometimes had bad dreams that frightened her, but never me. It was a long time before I fell asleep again.

Next day was bright and clear and windy. After breakfast we set out for the seashore, half a mile away. Meg was interested in seabirds, and Mrs. McLellan told her we would see some rare ones if we watched. The stony beach was deserted, and we sat at the water's edge and pulled off our trainers to dabble our feet. It was surprisingly warm, and so clear we could see tiny crabs running below, and strands of green and brown weed moving like flags in the current, twining round the rocks. Flocks of wild duck bobbed on the waves. To the east a little river, Machrie Water, gurgled in a narrow channel into the quiet sea. I had never been in such a peaceful spot. I began to relax.

"I do love it here," Meg said. "It could be a Stone Age beach, Ross, couldn't it?"

A warning bell rang in my mind. Stone—the Stones . . . I shivered, although I wasn't cold, and lay back and shut my eyes. I felt tired, and that was rare for me. What *was* the matter with me—was I starting scarlet fever myself?

"You do like it, don't you?" Meg said anxiously. She set great store by my opinion.

"Yes, of course," I said, and rolled on to my stomach. I didn't want to talk. Meg chattered on, about all the things we could do, climb the hills, go on the bus to Brodick, how we must send cards to Mum and tell her how beautiful it was here. I listened. I felt far away from her, as if I was turning into somebody different. I rolled a smooth, heavy stone in my hand, and thought of hunting red deer, running after them with a handful of stones, and that was strange, for I hated all forms of hunting.

As we walked back to the croft for dinner, Meg caught sight of the stones. The sun was glinting on them, and they looked silvery, innocent. "Oh, Ross, shall we go and look?" she said.

I set my jaw. "Don't be daft, it's dinner time. They're only old stones."

"Your voice sounds funny," Meg said, peering sideways at me. "I know they're only stones, but they're fascinating. Somebody must have put them there, centuries ago. What for, do you think?"

"I don't know and I don't care," I said, taking her arm and lugging her along. "Come on, I want my dinner."

But while we ate, Meg had to question Mrs. McLellan about the stones. Mrs. McLellan was evasive, I thought. Nobody knew much about the stones, she said. She didn't like them herself, and never went near them. "A burying place, some say that's what they are," she said. She cut us slices of fruit pie, and paused before she added: "They're best left to themselves. Sandy, our old dog, never goes nigh them."

"One's much bigger than all the rest, isn't it?" said Meg.

Again the hesitation. "That's the King Stone," Mrs. McLellan answered quietly. "Now help yourselves to some of my custard."

I reached out for the jug, and saw that my fingers were trembling. The King Stone—a good name for him. Why did I think of the stone as him, not it? I felt a wave of panic. I wanted to jump up and shout: "I hate them, I hate them all, and I can't get them out of my mind!" I swallowed, feeling half choked.

Mrs. McLellan was looking at me curiously. "You'll break the handle," she said, and took the jug from me.

I saw Meg look at me, her brow wrinkled, and then she looked down at her plate and didn't say another word. Sometimes she can guess what I'm thinking pretty accurately. At least she didn't mention the stones again, and that was a huge relief.

We caught the bus to Brodick that afternoon, and I was thankful to be among prosaic people and things. We did some shopping for Mrs. McLellan, explored the village and the harbour, and chose some postcards. Meg spent ages spinning round a holder full of cards, choosing with infinite care. I never bother much over things like that, so I took a few at random without looking. Standing there outside the shop in the spring sunshine, with people chattering round me, and children clanking buckets and spades, I looked at the three I had chosen, and went very cold. Each one was of the stones on Machrie Moor. I knew then there was no escape. On each card the King Stone leapt up at me. I addressed them, scribbled a few phrases and posted them straight away, to get them out of my hands.

That night in bed I read for a long time, and kept my back turned to the window. I didn't want to go to sleep, but at last, well after midnight, my eyes were aching so much I had to put the book down. I reached out and switched off the light. A strange half-darkness filled the room as I drifted uneasily off to sleep.

Again the nightmare came, as I knew it would, and it was worse this time. The stones were nearer, and the King Stone was gigantic. His mossy, uneven surface sparkled, giving him a strange grimace. His stone shoulders spread wide, blocking out the light. In the dream I was backing away, but my bare feet were dragging and I could scarcely lift them. The stone was breathing, he was alive, throbbing, and from him came the words: "You know you must come to me. I am waiting, I am tired of waiting. Come!"

I gasped: "No!" and with an unspeakable effort I forced myself to wake up.

To my horror a huge shape loomed over me, wavering. This was worse than the dream. I almost screamed. Then I saw it was the shadow cast by moonlight of the flapping curtain. I lay quivering, taking great gulping breaths to steady myself. I was so scared I almost rushed into Meg's room. But of course I didn't. I was always the one who looked after her, not the other way round. The last thing I wanted was to scare her as well. It's all in my mind, I told myself. It must be. The trouble was, I knew in my bones that wasn't true. Something implacably evil was after me, from the long ago, and it was getting closer.

When I woke up, and the bright sunshine was flooding through the thin curtains, I resolved not to mess about any longer, but to take some action. I would have to go to the King Stone, though the mere thought made me shudder. But I had to do it, because it was the only way out of this frightening maze. I'll go, and touch the stone, and maybe that will make everything normal and sane again, I thought.

A stone can't be alive, can't have power. I'll go today, and prove it.

But when? I knew I had to go alone, and Meg wanted us to go out for the day, exploring the caves near Black-waterfoot, the next village. Mrs. McLellan had promised to pack us a big picnic lunch, and it was all arranged. Well, I would have to go that night, that was all.

We tramped along the beach to the caves, and I felt much better and more like myself, the further we got away from Machrie Moor. We met nobody else, and sang loud nonsense songs that set the gulls shrieking indignantly, and threw flat stones into the sea to make them skim. Meg beamed on me occasionally and seemed pleased.

"This is fun, isn't it, Ross? It's a perfect holiday," she said, as we sprawled eating our sandwiches in the sunshine. "P'raps we can come again some time with Mum."

"No, thanks," I said brusquely. "I'd rather go somewhere else."

"I wish you'd tell me what's worrying you," Meg said.

"What rubbish. Don't be crazy," I said.

"But, Ross, I might be able to help——" she began beseechingly.

"Shut up!" I snapped. "Shut *up*!" I rarely shouted at her, and I felt mean, but I had to. How could I tell her about the stones, and the way they were haunting me? It would only worry and scare her.

After that the day was spoilt. We reached the caves and explored them, and then wandered round the village at Blackwaterfoot, but we said little to each other. As a peace-offering, I asked Meg if she'd like an ice, but she refused, and by mid-afternoon we had turned back towards Machrie Moor. With every step, the terror came back to me.

It was a question of killing time now, waiting until I could go to the stones. We played cards with the McLellans all evening, and I tried to throw myself into it. The clock hands moved slowly onwards, and all too soon it was ten o'clock, and we all went up to bed.

There was a full moon rising, brightening in the sky as the daylight faded. I sat by the window watching the darkness come creeping across the moor. At midnight I would go. I was full of a strange exaltation now. Why had I felt so scared? I had to go—it was the right thing. The house was utterly still when at last I went slowly down the creaky stairs. Nothing could have stopped me.

I unlocked the door and closed it gently behind me, and went steadily on to the stones. They seemed nearer the house, to be beckoning me. The moonlight poured peacefully down on them, and their long, crooked shadows slanted across the moor towards me. The longest shadow came from the King Stone. I felt at peace now. Steadily I walked on into the circle, and came right up to the stone. I stood in the circle facing the King Stone.

"You see, I've come. I'm not afraid," I said, and laid both hands on the cold rough surface.

Then, in a flash, everything changed. My hands clung to the King Stone, and I couldn't tear them away. The King Stone was pulling me closer, hanging on to me. He had got me! And round the others there were people dressed in skins, some carrying blazing torches, chanting and dancing. The noise was overwhelming. They were dancing round the stones, round and round, and gradually and relentlessly they drew nearer till they were dancing round the King Stone alone. Smoke from the torches singed my eyes, the loud chanting deafened me, the faces flashing past, nearer and nearer to me, were lit up in the glare, full of excitement, snarling with anticipation. There was no pity in any of them. I struggled to pull myself away, but the power of the King Stone bound me, as if I was tied up in ropes. Then I saw a tall, dark-skinned man move very near, still chanting as he raised his spear. I saw how it shone in the moonlight, especially the jaggedly sharp pointed tip. And I knew all this had happened to me once before, long, long ago. The savage, contorted face, the blazing eyes, the burnished spear, I remembered everything now. In a moment I would lie dead at the foot of the merciless King Stone, and he would at last be satisfied. There was nothing I could do, nobody to help me.

I felt utterly lonely. The stars above me spun jerkily as I lifted my head, trying freziedly to pull away. The moon reeled before my eyes. Then, as the spear flashed down towards my chest, I fainted. It was no us trying any more. It was all over. The King Stone had triumphed.

"Ross! Ross!"

It was Meg's voice, from another world. Slowly, reluctantly, I drifted back to consciousness. I was lying in the grass beyond the stone circle where she must have dragged me, and she was kneeling over me, crying and shaking me.

"Oh, Ross, do wake up—*please!*"

I sat up very slowly, realising the spear had never reached me. The night was perfectly still, so still I could hear the waves washing on the beach half a mile away, and there was only Meg and myself. Her face was chalky white in the moonlight.

"I heard you come downstairs, and I came after you. I knew there was something wrong. Oh, Ross, are you all

B

right? Why were you twisting about against the stone like that?"

"Didn't you see them all?" I said dazedly, but I knew she hadn't.

"I had to pull and pull to get you away from the King Stone. I was scared, but I knew something awful would happen if I didn't. You looked dreadful! And suddenly the stone let you go." She was shivering. "Oh, Ross, let's get away from them!"

I stood up, and my legs felt like jelly. "Tomorrow we'll make some excuse and get away from the island—go home," I whispered shakily. "They'll always be waiting for me while I stay—especially *him*. I can't explain, Meg, but we must."

Blessedly, Meg didn't ask any questions, simply nodded in acceptance, and squeezed my icy hand.

We walked back towards the croft, keeping well away from the stones. But the power had gone, and even the King Stone, when I dared to glance at him, had lost his malevolence. Or had he? Was it a trick? Hand in hand we reached the croft door, and looked back. The stones seemed to have shrunk, to be sleeping in the moonlight. They had lost for now.

But I knew too well they would always be waiting for me. Always, till the end of my life.

TOM

by FRANK RICHARDS

"HAVE you seen that dog Mr. Dunham has got?" asked Jane's mother.

"No," said Jane, "I can't say that I have."

"Have you seen it, dear?" she asked her husband.

Mr. Carter finished his tea and put down the cup. "I should think I have," he said. "What an animal!"

Jane loved dogs and was immediately interested. "What's it like?"

"It's a big, black thing," said her father. "Monstrous! Everyone in the village is talking about it."

"What breed is it?"

"Heaven knows. It's the biggest mongrel ever born. Looks a vicious brute."

"Oh, I'm sure it isn't," said Mrs. Carter. "You always have this idea about dogs."

"Well, I wouldn't like to take any chances with it. It'd probably have your throat out."

The conversation continued as it always did at mealtimes. The evening routine went on. Jane did her homework, watched telly for a bit, had a cup of cocoa and went to bed. She couldn't help thinking about the dog and was fascinated by her father's description. Was it really as vicious as he made out? He always exaggerated things. Anyhow, next day was Saturday; she'd take a walk down to the village to find out for herself.

She got up early next morning, and went out to fetch a few things from the village shop. The Carters lived just outside the Norfolk village where they had moved just a year before. Jane had soon been captivated by the flat, charming countryside of East Anglia, and felt that she was one of the natives by this time.

It was a lovely summer's morning, and there was a light breeze blowing from the sea, three miles away. She felt very happy.

She got the things from the shop, and looked round for Mr. Dunham. He lived not far from them, and they had met several times already. But perhaps he would be working this morning; after all, he was a farmer.

Then she realised her luck was in, for coming round the side of "The Blue Boar" were Mr. Dunham and his dog. Yes, it was a large animal; a monstrous dog, almost the size of a Great Dane, Jane thought. It walked at Mr. Dunham's heels at a gentle pace.

She watched as a woman with a small boy passed the pair, and was surprised and amused to see her step out into the road and protectively put the child on the other side of her as they passed the dog.

Jane drew near to the farmer. "Good morning, Mr. Dunham."

" 'Morning, Jane," he replied with that curious East Anglian drawl. "Doing a bit of shopping?"

"Yes, that's right. Is this the dog I've heard so much about?"

"Yes, there's been a lot of talk, I believe. It's a pity some folk haven't something better to gossip about."

"Why? What have they said about him?"

"They reckon he's vicious."

The dog had stopped by its master and now sat on the pavement with a bored expression.

"And isn't he?"

"Certainly not. He's like a kitten; ain't you, Tom?"

The dog looked up and responded with a half-wag of its tail.

"He looks quite nice." Although Jane said this, she wasn't really sure. The dog had some strange look about it—particularly the eyes, that burned deep, appearing to hide some dark secret that Jane couldn't understand.

"He's all right. He's a good working dog," went on the farmer. "And he's a good watch-dog. I'd hate to be anybody who broke into my place while he was about."

So would I, thought Jane. "Where did you get him from?" she asked.

"Ah, now," said Mr. Dunham. "That's the odd thing about it. Do you remember that big storm we had about a fortnight ago—where the thunder rolled all night and the lightning made it like day?"

"Yes, I remember."

"Well, I kept going outside to see if the ricks were all right, and there he sat in the rain. I swear he wasn't there twenty minutes before. I shall never forget the lightning flashing in his eyes. Well, as I say, there sat poor old Tom —wet through. I couldn't leave him outside on a night like that, so I took him in. But where he came from I haven't any idea. Nobody has ever claimed him, so I reckon I'm stuck with him, ain't I, Tom?"

"May I stroke him?" asked Jane.

"Yes, go on. He won't mind."

She leant forward cautiously and stroked the great head; she still wasn't sure of him. Once again there was that one half-wag of the tail and nothing more. It seemed to be an automatic action, and Jane was disappointed. Most dogs looked pleased when you stroked them, and put their heads up for more, but not this one. She looked into his eyes again, and still that far-away, hidden secret burned within them.

"Well . . . well," she said, hardly sure of her words. "Yes, Mr. Dunham, he's a very nice dog. I must be getting along now. Goodbye."

"Goodbye, Jane. Come on, Tom. Let's get back."

She watched the man and the dog amble slowly up the street, her mind still full of the strange animal.

"I saw that dog," she said at dinner-time.

"Did you?" said her father. "What did you think about it?"

"It was all right," she replied, not very enthusiastically. "Big one, isn't it?"

"You be careful."

"Why? Mr. Dunham was there."

"Well . . . yes . . . but be careful," he repeated.

She saw Mr. Dunham and his dog once or twice after that, and the ritual was always the same: the pat on the head, the half-hearted wag of the tail, and the deep fire burning in the eyes. She admired the dog as a fine specimen, but found herself secretly agreeing with half the village: it was a strange dog—and perhaps a dangerous one. She just didn't know.

About a week later, Mr. Martin was in the house. Something had gone wrong with the central heating, and he was the local plumber. He was a Norfolk man of over sixty and, like most older people in the country, he took life very leisurely. Consequently, after his work was finished, he sat drinking tea with them in the kitchen.

All sorts of things were discussed: the crops, the weather, the village fête, and then it turned—as Jane knew it would—to Dunham's dog. Mr. Martin shared the opinion of most people.

"A very weird dog," he said, shaking his head. "I said to Bert Dunham, 'What do you want a dog like that for, Bert? If it was a sheep-dog or something I could understand it, but that thing looks more like a shuck to me. Are you sure you ain't got an old black shuck there?'"

"What's a shuck?" asked Mrs. Carter and Jane together.

"You can tell they're not Norfolk born and bred, can't you, Mr. Martin?" said Mr. Carter.

"Why? Do *you* know, Dad?" asked Jane.

"Yes, but let Mr. Martin tell you. He knows all about shucks."

"A shuck," said Mr. Martin gravely. "It's a phantom dog. It's big and black and haunts lonely roads at night."

Jane shivered. "How horrible. Do they do any harm?"

"They're said to do terrible things. Frighten people to death."

38

"Oh, come," said Mr. Carter. "Surely no one takes them seriously these days."

"I ain't so sure about that. When I was a lad I heard a lot of old people talk about them. No one would go out alone through the lanes at night. More than one old chap I knew swore that he'd seen them."

"Big and black . . ." said Jane, thinking about Tom.

"Big and black with great red eyes, glowing like fire. Just like Bert Dunham's dog. So that's what I said. 'I reckon you've got a shuck there, Bert'." He picked up his cap to go. "Well, I reckon I've done enough talking here. Thanks for the tea, Mrs. Carter. It's getting dark. I'd better be off now or I'll have the shucks after me." He chuckled, and with a cheery wave of his hand he was gone.

"Was he really joking?" asked Jane.

"My dear girl," said her father, "if you're going to listen to every story old people round here tell you, you'll never stop worrying. Interesting, but a load of superstitious rubbish. I'll tell you one thing, though—I'd sooner have a shuck after me than Mr. Dunham's dog, so there."

A fortnight later, Jane was sitting with Carol, one of her schoolfriends, at Carol's house. She had been to a party there. All the others had gone. They lived in the opposite direction from Jane, and Carol's father had taken them home in his car. Afterwards, he was going to Norwich to meet a relative off the late train. Jane's father was to fetch her. The phone rang, and Carol's mother went to answer it.

"It's for you, Jane," she called.

Jane walked into the hall and picked up the phone.

"Jane?" said her mother's voice. "Some bad news, I'm afraid. The car won't start. I know it's asking a lot, but can Carol's father bring you home?"

"No, Mummy. He's gone off to Norwich."

"Oh dear. Then what are you going to do? Shall we walk out to meet you?"

"No, don't bother, I'll walk home on my own. It's only

a couple of miles, and it isn't ten yet. I shall be home in half an hour."

"All right, dear, but be careful."

"What have I got to be frightened about? Shucks or something?"

Her mother gave a nervous laugh and put down the phone.

As Jane said her goodbyes and thank-yous at the door, she stepped into the fading light, and wished she hadn't said anything about shucks. The night was fine, but there was that stiff breeze blowing, making the clouds race across the moon.

She set out at a brisk pace, the thoughts of the terrible black dogs running through her mind. She tried to think of other things—pleasant things, things about her home and the village, but her mind always went round in a circle and ended up with Tom, that great, mysterious dog. Why did she keep thinking about him? "Looks like a shuck to me," Mr. Martin had said. She shivered and broke into a faster walk.

She went along familiar roads and lanes; after all, it wasn't as if she were lost. She felt happier on the main road with the cars going by; then she turned into a narrow, dark lane, bounded by trees and a low hedge.

There were eerie shadows all about her. The clouds still swept across the moon; an owl hooted; a cock-pheasant made her jump as it flew up from the roadside. Then she heard something. It was a howl—a blood-curdling howl like that of a wolf. It seemed to fill the whole night sky. It was some distance away, but it sent shivers down her spine. Then silence. She walked on.

There came another. Much nearer this time, on the other side of the road. Oh, why hadn't she waited for Dad to come and meet her?

Then she heard a curious noise. It was quite soft at first. It sounded like someone or something panting very quickly. She turned. There was nothing. The sound seemed to be following her, getting steadily louder.

It was soon joined by another sound: the pad, pad, pad of feet, like the paws of an animal. It appeared to be at the side of the road, moving at a constant speed. Very frightened by this time, she turned and saw a dark shape by the hedge. All was silent except for the panting and the incessant pad, pad, pad. She began to cry a little. Wasn't there a phone box about? But there was no phone; not even a house in sight.

She stopped. The panting stopped. The padding ceased. Absolute silence again. Then, as the moon came out from behind the clouds, she saw the black shape clearly. There it stood, a dog, a huge dog, black as the night that surrounded it. Only two things shone out in the darkness—its eyes that glowed like fire, and the white of its teeth bared in a snarl.

She screamed and ran. It was useless. The thing still kept up with her, but it did not appear to be running. It still kept up its regular pad, pad, pad. Almost faint with fear, she stumbled on. The rhythm of the pad then seemed to change its pattern. The panting was quicker. She looked about her as the horrible truth dawned. There were two of them! Another had appeared on the other side of the road. With a desperate effort she turned to face them, and screamed again. What good would that do? There they were on each side of her—silent, red eyes gleaming, and white teeth shining in the scanty moonlight.

She was overcome by panic, and ran blindly along the middle of the road. Then she stopped suddenly, for this surely was the end! Another dog stood there, barring her path. She sank down whimpering into the road, praying for help. All three dogs stood silent and still. She looked up at the dog facing her. There was something different about this one, for she recognized it. It was Tom. There he stood, looking even bigger than she's seen him before. His hair stood on end and his eyes burned brightly with that hidden fire. Mr. Martin's words came back again. "I reckon you've a shuck there." Yes, it was true. He was right.

A huge dog, black as the night . . .

And then a curious truth struck her. Tom was not looking at her at all; he was staring intently at one of the two creatures at the side of the road. He advanced, passing her unheeded, looking twice his normal size, stiff-legged, tall and terrible in the moonlight. Then his head went down, guarding his throat as dogs do when they fight. With a low growl he walked on unhesitatingly towards the beast on his right. Suddenly he leapt. There was a brief scuffle, a high-pitched howl, and the creature vanished like mist. It had not run over the fields, nor down the road; it had just disappeared. The other black shape still lurked in the hedge-row, and as Tom turned in its direction, Jane felt her fear ebbing away, giving way to a kind of excitement. She watched transfixed as the phantom stood its ground against this terrible opponent.

Tom was within a foot of it now, his growls assuming a more menacing tone. The beast decided that retreat was the better proposition. For the first time it ran—ran into an adjoining field with Tom in close pursuit. Jane saw both of them disappear behind a haystack, then she heard that blood-curdling howl again, but it had no fear for her this time. It was a howl of pain and terror. Then there was nothing: nothing but the moon and the night and the silence. From behind the haystack came Tom.

He walked over to her. "Good boy, Tom," she whispered.

The dog nuzzled his head against her side, and she stroked his head. The tail was wagging—not the half-hearted wag she had seen in the village, but the action of an animal that is pleased with what it has done.

They walked home together, she with her hand on the huge creature's back. Her fear had completely gone now. Who could harm her with this great champion by her side? Whatever those creatures had been—dogs or ghosts—nothing could touch her now.

Tom left her at the end of the village. As she walked into the house and greeted her relieved mother, Jane decided not to mention the shucks. Her mother would only worry, and her father would accuse her of having too much imagination. No, it was better to let dogs, sleeping or otherwise, lie.

She often saw her new friend in the street after that: still the old fire burnt in the eyes, still the half-wag of the tail. And still she wondered at the secrets that were locked tight in that great black head. One thing, however, was certain. She would never again walk those Norfolk lanes alone at night. Dear old Tom might not be there the next time.

THE LAVENDER LADY

by VALERIE WATERS

SIMON and Debbie Lister noticed nothing strange about Lavender Cottage when they first saw it one morning in May.

"What a lovely house!" declared Debby as the car came to a standstill outside it. "How old do you think it is?"

"It's Tudor, of course," said Simon crushingly. He was eleven, nearly two years older than Debbie, and had studied the Tudors at school, so he knew all about their houses.

The cottage was indeed very charming, with its white-washed walls and black beams, the diamond panes of the casement windows sparkling in the bright sunshine.

Mr. Lister was already humping the cases along the stone-flagged path, bordered by the grey-green bushes of lavender that had given the cottage its name.

"Simon," called his mother, "come and help me with Jeremy."

Simon obediently grasped one handle of the carrycot which contained his baby brother. Jeremy stretched out a fat, pink hand towards the blossom on the apple tree outside the front door, gurgling contentedly.

"Jerry likes his new home, doesn't he?" commented Debbie, leaning over the carrycot as it was placed on the chintz-covered settee in the long, low-ceilinged sitting-room.

"And so do I," she went on, running to look out of the window. "I'm so glad Dad has a new job here. I've always wanted to live in Somerset, ever since I heard that old song: 'Green Hills of Somerset'. They really are so very green—and such funny shapes."

45

She gazed through the window at the humpy, hillocky mounds that seemed to surround the little market town of Somerville.

"Oh, stop mooning about, Deb," said Simon crisply. "You're always dreaming about something." And their mother joined in with: "Yes, children, time to unpack your things before we have tea."

As Debbie was carefully arranging her collection of Whimsies on the broad wooden windowsill of her room, she heard Simon calling her from the next room.

"Can you smell something unusual in here?" he asked.

Debbie sniffed, puzzled for a moment. Then:

"Lavender," she said. "This is called Lavender Cottage, you know."

"But the strange thing is," persisted Simon, "the lavender isn't out yet. I noticed as we came in."

Simon was always winning prizes at school for being observant, so Debbie didn't argue.

"I expect someone's been using lavender polish. Mum does sometimes."

They thought no more about it till the next morning, then, while Mrs. Lister was in the middle of unpacking their books and putting them in the bookcase, Jeremy began to cry.

"Go and rock the pram for me, please, Debbie," she said. "It's not time for Jerry's feed yet."

As Debbie went down the path, she noticed to her surprise that the pram was already rocking—but there was no wind, the branches of the cherry tree above the pram were hanging limply still in the warm air. Jeremy had stopped crying.

"He must be making the pram rock himself," thought Debbie, but when she bent over it, Jeremy was lying quite still with a wide smile on his face, holding out his arms to be picked up.

"Up you come, then," said Debbie, lifting him out.

The baby's blue eyes seemed to be looking at something behind his sister's right shoulder and, although there were no lavender plants in the back garden, the same faint fragrance she had smelled the evening before drifted to her nostrils.

Debbie turned her head towards the scent. The air seemed to be curiously thicker just behind her shoulder, almost a shape, like drifting smoke from a bonfire. Debbie closed her eyes, and for a moment she seemed to see quite clearly a young woman in a long print gown, her hair drawn back and coiled into a glossy chestnut bun.

Debbie thought she had never before seen a beautiful face look so sad. The picture was so vivid that she opened her eyes expecting the vision to be still there, but there was nothing. Even the scent of lavender had gone.

"Simon," said Debbie, when they were getting ready for bed that night, "would you think I was silly if I said I think there's a ghost in this cottage?"

She waited for him to laugh.

"No," said Simon unexpectedly. "I can feel there's— something strange here. Tell me about it, Deb."

After that, they both noticed little signs of what they came to call the Lavender Lady every day; the smell of lavender, the way the keys on the piano moved up and down occasionally, as if someone was playing an unheard tune, the rocking of the pram when no one was near.

All these things happened only near Jeremy, who seemed able to see someone invisible to them, and they never happened when Mr. and Mrs. Lister were around, although occasionally, if Debbie closed her eyes, she saw again the image of the unhappy young woman in the strange dress. It was as if the ghost was only interested in children, and particularly in Jeremy.

"Do you think we ought to tell Mummy?" Debbie asked.

Simon answered firmly: "No, I don't. You know what grown-ups are like, even sensible ones like Mum and Dad. They'd only laugh."

"Perhaps you're right," said Debbie. "But why do you

47

think I'm the only one to see the ghost—except for Jeremy, I mean? Why don't you?"

"I don't know. I sort of—feel her there. I think you must be what they call extra perceptive—E.S.P., or something. Remember the time you told Dad how frightened you were in that old church, and then the verger told us about it being haunted by a wicked organist?"

Debbie nodded.

"And we won't tell Mum and Dad then. The Lavender Lady doesn't seem to be doing any harm to Jeremy."

But they were soon to change their minds. In the weeks that followed, as the lavender came shyly into bloom, Jeremy began suddenly to lose his appetite, pushing away the spoon with his favourite strained fruit in it, and drinking hardly any of his milk. His face lost its healthy tan from the summer sun, his chubby arms and legs grew thin. Although before he had been struggling to sit up in his pram, he now seemed content just to lie there.

Mrs. Lister, worried and frightened, took the baby to the doctor, who examined him thoroughly, but could find no cause for Jeremy's listlessness.

The next afternoon, Debbie and Simon were looking down at their little brother in the pram under the cherry tree and were trying, by tickling his ribs, to make him smile as he used to do. But Jeremy lay quite still, his eyes always fixed on something beyond them. The elusive lavender scent hung in the air.

"Simon," whispered Debbie in horror, "it's as if we were the ghosts, not her. But why should the Lavender Lady want to hurt Jerry? Her face looks so kind. We must find out more about her."

"We'll ask the vicar," decided Simon. "He's sure to know about any ghost, and when he called to welcome us he did say he'd be glad if we'd visit him some time."

So after tea they went along to the old grey vicarage, where the vicar, Mr. Astbury, pink-faced and plumpish, greeted them with a warm smile.

"A ghost at the cottage?" he said comfortably, ramming

tobacco into his pipe. "Well, there is one rather sad story about a young Victorian girl, called Lilian Lavenham. It seems she fell in love with a wild young man her parents didn't approve of, a sailor, so she ran off and married him against their will. A very pretty girl she was too, by all accounts."

A picture of that lovely face and chestnut hair swam into Debbie's mind.

"What happened then?" she demanded.

"Not long after their marriage, her husband was drowned at sea. Lilian was expecting a baby by then and she had nowhere to go but back home. Her parents took her in, but when the baby was born, they took it away and refused even to let her know what became of it."

"How cruel!" Debbie exclaimed indignantly.

"The poor girl never really recovered from it. Apparently she used to wander round the village looking in all the prams for her lost baby, and a few years later both she and her parents died in a 'flu epidemic."

"Thank you very much, Mr. Astbury," said Simon, getting up and urging Debbie towards the door.

"Going so soon?" asked the vicar. He looked at them keenly. "If you want my help any time, you've only to ask."

"What is it, Simon?" asked Debbie, as soon as they were outside.

"Don't you see!" hissed Simon. "Lilian wants to have Jeremy to take the place of her own baby, and, as she's dead, she wants him to die too."

"To die! Oh, Simon, what shall we do?"

"We must tell Mum and Dad, get them to leave Lavender Cottage before it's too late."

But, as he had feared earlier, Mr. and Mrs. Lister brushed aside their story.

"Of course Jerry is ill," said their mother kindly," and you're worried, but I'm taking him to the specialist's in a few days' time. He'll find out what's the matter. Ghost, indeed! You've been reading too many horror stories."

"It may be too late in a few days' time," wailed Debbie as they sat in Simon's room.

"Look, Deb, let's just sit quietly and think. This room always seems to be more haunted than the others, as if somebody was trying to get through to us. Perhaps it was hers—Lilian's, I mean. See if you can feel anything special."

They sat in silence for about ten minutes. Debbie's eyes closed, and her breathing became soft and regular. Then she suddenly rose from her chair with her hands out in front of her, as if she were sleepwalking. She went straight to the old chimney place, reached inside, and in a moment produced an old tin box, very cracked and covered with soot. Then she seemed to come to herself and stood staring down at the box with wonder.

"What's in it, Debbie?" asked Simon eagerly.

Inside were neatly parcelled papers that seemed to be marriage and birth certificates. Underneath was a faded sepia photograph of a young girl with a cameo brooch pinned to the neck of her starched blouse. It was the Lavender Lady.

At the bottom of the box was a black notebook, filled with beautiful copperplate handwriting. It appeared to be a journal of some kind, written by a Josiah Lavenham, and the pages fell open of their own accord at a place in the middle.

"This night," read Simon slowly, "my daughter Lilian was delivered of a male child, that died the same night. We buried the infant, without benefit of clergy, in the back garden by the lilac tree, and marked the place by a stone. Let it be my daughter's punishment, for defying the wishes of her parents, never to know what became of it."

The two children sat staring at each other, then, without a word, dashed together into the garden. The purple lilac was still in the corner by the fence, and they pushed their way towards it through the overgrown shrubs. Gently parting the drooping leaves, they found beneath it an old grey paving stone, yellowed at the edges with lichen, set into the soil.

"So her baby was here all the time," murmured Debbie. "Poor Lilian." She paused thoughtfully. "But what does 'without benefit of clergy' mean?"

"I think it means without a proper burial service spoken by a clergyman. Perhaps that was why Lilian was never able to find her baby, even after she died."

"And I think," put in Debbie, "that her parents are sorry now for what they did and helped me to find that notebook. But what do we do now?"

"Fetch Mr. Astbury. He'll know what to do."

After hearing their story, Mr. Astbury came back with them at once. Debbie rushed upstairs to Jeremy's cot, where she addressed the unseen presence still hovering nearby.

"Miss Lilian, we know now where your own baby is. Will you follow me, please?"

The floating scent of lavender accompanied them to the lilac tree, where Mr. Astbury, with bowed head, said the words of the Burial Service over the grey stone.

"Both their souls should be at peace now," said the vicar.

Simon and Debbie rushed back indoors to the cot. Jeremy's blue eyes looked directly at them for the first time in weeks, and he held out his arms towards them, crying the cry of a normal, hungry baby.

"Mummy! Mummy!" Debbie yelled, as she carried her brother downstairs to a delighted Mrs. Lister. "Jerry's better."

"Better go and thank Lilian," said Simon.

They pushed their way back through the shrubs. There was no trace in the atmosphere of the ghost's presence, but there on the stone lay three sprigs of freshly-picked lavender.

MAGIC ON THE FIELD

by EVE GOTHARD

GERRY sprawled on his bed, staring wearily at the posters of football teams pinned up all around the walls. Largest of all, and nearest his bed, was one of Birmingham City, the team he supported tenaciously through all their triumphs and disasters. He gazed at all the confident, smiling faces, and sighed. If *only* he could get into the school team, like his dad years ago, and play against the Killers in the vital match that was coming up soon. Why couldn't he manage it?

"I try and try, but I can't make it," he muttered, kicking at his quilt.

The others teased him because he was small for his age, and called him Titch, which made him mad. What was so funny about being small? You didn't have to be a giant to be a good footballer. He wanted to be a striker, and it was speed that counted with them, not size. Everyone knew that who knew *anything*. Passionately he longed to be in the school team with Ginger, Dave and the others. Football counted for a lot at Fairfield Junior. Photos of past school teams hung dominatingly around the school hall. The school had a great reputation for it. Gerry was ten and a half, and had only one more year at Fairfield. If he didn't make it soon, he never would.

"You can only do your best, Gerry," Froggy had told him today in a friendly way. This was after a practice when Gerry had worked himself nearly into the ground but still knew he hadn't played really well. Froggy was Mr. Froggett, who had been sports teacher at Fairfield for donkeys' years. He'd even taught Gerry's dad. He was going bald, but he could still run as fast as any of the boys, and he never seemed to get tired. "You work hard at football, I know, son, but you need a bit of natural talent as well. It'll probably come, so give it time, and don't look so down. Rome wasn't built in a day, remember."

What had Rome got to do with it? Grown-ups were always saying daft things like that. Gerry glumly rolled over on his stomach. He knew how much his dad wanted to see him in the team. *He'd* been one of the stars.

"Come on, Gerry," his mum called up briskly. "Tea's ready. Wash your hands. Don't forget, like you usually do!"

"Coming, Mum." Gerry slowly slid off the bed, aiming a sliced kick at an imaginary football en route to the door. "A great goal!" he said under his breath. "The fans cheered wildly as the ball hit the back of the net like a rocket."

"Gerry—get a move on!"

"Oh, all *right*." Gerry went reluctantly into the bathroom, gave his hands the briefest possible wash, without bothering to look at them, and jumped down the stairs.

In the kitchen his mother, dishing him up baked beans and sausages, said resignedly: "You went up there to change, remember?"

"Thought I'd go down to the school field again after tea, just for half an hour. Froggy said I could," said Gerry. "Thanks, Mum."

His mother eyed him. "Don't you ever think of anything but football? You're enough to drive anyone crazy. It's not the only thing in life, you know."

Gerry concentrated on eating. His mother got sick of football. he knew, and it was no good arguing about it.

After finishing a large tea he put on his football boots again, picked up the muddy ball kept permanently by the back door, and slipped through a hole in the hedge into the school playing field. It was a handy short cut he often used. He could get to school in two minutes flat, that way.

It was a grey, gloomy evening. Nobody else was about, and all the school buildings were locked up and deserted.

Gerry didn't mind—he preferred practising on his own. It was better without the others being stupid, calling him Titch and pretending they couldn't see him. Just because they were bigger, they thought they were so clever . . . Especially Ginger. Gerry liked Ginger, but he was always taking the mickey. Oh well! He decided to practise heading. He wasn't much good at it, and he always messed it up. He began doggedly throwing the ball into the air. Ouch, that hurt! He'd done it wrong again . . .

"You don't want to do it like that."

Gerry spun round crossly. A boy about his own age was standing there. Gerry had no idea where he'd come from. He was wearing rather baggy football shorts, and unfamiliar, heavy-looking boots. He had a pale, serious face, and he spoke in a grave, not bossy voice.

"I don't want you telling me how. I can do it," said Gerry truculently and untruthfully.

"Look, try like this," the boy said calmly. He tossed the ball up, then merely swerved his body as he touched it gently with his forehead and sent it flying. "Low down, see? Go on, try it like that. And sidestep your feet to shoot it past at an angle."

Gerry grudgingly did. After several attempts he got the hang of it, and felt cheered. "Thanks," he said, rather ashamed. "You're good at it."

"It's only practice," said the boy offhandedly.

Gerry looked at him. "Do you live near here? I've never seen you before." He was sure he would remember. He had never seen a boy with so many blotchy freckles.

The boy didn't answer. Well, some people didn't like questions. Gerry got sick of them himself. Instead, the boy said: "Want me to go in goal and you can try and shoot?"

"Great," said Gerry eagerly. His friends always wanted *him* to be goalie, and this was too good an offer to refuse.

"Come on, then." ￢

Silently they played, with great concentration. The boy was exceedingly light and quick on his feet. He leapt across the goal-mouth, punching or kicking like lightning at the ball. It was intensely difficult to get it past him—he was like a tiger—but Gerry managed it once or twice and felt triumphant. It was getting too dark to see now, though, and lights were coming on in the houses. Gerry said reluctantly: "We'll have to stop."

"Yep. You're not bad." The boy kicked the ball across the muddy grass to him.

"Thanks for the game. Maybe I'll see you again some time?" said Gerry hopefully.

"Maybe." The boy was turning away.

"What's your name?" Gerry called curiously. And floating across the dark field came the one word: "Phil". Then the boy was gone, lost in the darkness. Gerry ran back, feeling cold, scrambling through the hedge. Hope I see him again. He's a natural, he thought. And not big-headed, either!

Next morning, squashed between his friends at morning assembly, he sang the hymns lustily and felt cheerful again. Looking round as he always did at the pictures of the school football teams, from years ago, when his father played in defence, right up to last winter's, he thought more determinedly than ever: "I'll get in the team soon. I just *won't* give up, I'll practice every night after school. I won't tell anyone but I'll keep at it—and if Phil turns up again, that'll be great."

Perhaps because he was small, Gerry had learnt to be extra stubborn.

"Want to kick a ball around with us, Titch?" said Ginger, at going home time. "We're off to the park for an hour."

"No, thanks." Though he was flattered, Gerry was going to stick to his plan religiously.

Ginger was surprised. "Thought you were so keen?"

"He's gone off it, 'cos he's not got into the team," said Dave, grinning.

"I haven't, so you can just shut up," flared Gerry.

"Don't get steamed up, Titch," said Ginger maddeningly. "Kids ought to be polite."

Gerry debated whether to lash out, but decided against it. Ginger was so much heavier and taller, he'd be bound to get the worst of it. "I've got something better to do. Night," he said, and slipped away before they could ask any awkward questions. Just let them wait—he'd wipe those smiles off their faces!

After tea he slipped off to the school field again, and wondered if Phil would come. He practised dribbling up and down, carefully, concentrating with all his brain. Dribbling was important if you wanted to be any good as a striker. Up and down the field he went, the ball at his toes, weaving in and out past imaginary looming defenders.

"Hi."

It was Phil. He had turned up again as if from nowhere. It was funny—Gerry never saw him coming, but, anyhow, there he was.

"Hi. I hoped you'd come," said Gerry breathlessly.

"Like me to try tackling you?" Phil never wasted a word.

"You bet."

Again they settled to a strenuous routine, both totally absorbed.

So it went on, night after night that week. Gerry was steadily improving with the daily work-out. He could feel his game getting sharper, his feet more skilful. It was a lot because of Phil. He showed Gerry various skills that he could copy. He never spoke an unnecessary word, but Gerry knew he was as mad on football as he himself. They never spoke about anything else.

"D'you know St. Kenelm's—the Killers, they call themselves?" Gerry asked him at the end of one session.

Phil nodded. "They're the toughest round here to beat."

"I'll say! D'you play for a team anywhere?" Gerry felt he must.

"Used to." Phil was bending down, tightening his laces.

"Round here?"

After a pause: "Used to." Phil stood up again. "I'm going now." And he ran off into the gathering gloom.

56

Oh well! He was mysterious all right, but Gerry decided not to ask any more questions. What did it matter? So long as Phil kept coming, that was the important thing. He didn't want to put him off. He liked him a lot.

"Don't you get tired of playing over there on your own?" said his mother, when he came in tired out.

"Nope," said Gerry laconically. For some reason he didn't want to tell her about Phil. She'd be curious to see him, probably tell Gerry to bring him in for a drink and a biscuit, and Phil wouldn't want to, Gerry knew that.

His mother sighed. "You're a funny boy."

Next morning his dad said at breakfast: "Your mother tells me you're practising over in the field every night, Gerry." He hesitated. "That's good, but don't be too down if you're not picked, O.K.?"

"O.K., Dad." Gerry scrunched a mouthful of cornflakes, then said: "How old were you when you played for Fairfield, Dad?"

"I forget—about your age."

"Was it a good side, when you were in it?"

"Not bad, son." His father leant back, a far-away look in his eyes. "We could beat most sides round here, but you know the one we most wanted to beat? St. Kenelm's."

"Yeah, it's still the same. Kenelm's the rotten old Killers," Gerry said. "You know they beat us before Christmas—well, we've got the return match next Monday, and we've *got* to win or they'll never let us forget it!"

"I might come and cheer you on," his father said. "You need all the help you can get, playing them. When will the team be picked?"

"Froggy's going to choose after practice today," Gerry said. He laid down his spoon, feeling rather sick. He had been working towards this, but now he felt scared inside.

"Nice bloke, Froggy," his father said reminiscently, "though he must be getting on a bit now."

Gerry grinned, remembering something. "He remembers you scoring an own goal, Dad."

57

"I deny it." His father got up and ruffled Gerry's hair on his way to the garage. "Good luck, old son."

"You two are as bad as each other," Gerry's mother said, but she was smiling. "A couple of fanatics!"

Mr. Froggett was on his toes at the practice that afternoon. He ran tirelessly about the field in his shabby old tracksuit, whistle slung around his neck, watching everyone intently.

He had to admit he was astonished at Gerry Holt's improvement. The boy had always been as keen as mustard, trying painfully hard, but now he had suddenly from nowhere acquired a style of his own. He was moving well, much more swiftly and purposefully, getting on to the ball and hanging on to it. He was certainly a lightweight, but he had a lot of guts and wasn't scared of hard knocks. The kid must have put in hours of work on his own. And there was something about the way he was heading the ball with a twist and a flick that reminded Froggy of somebody else, way back in the past. Was it his father? No, he remembered him clearly enough: a solid, chunky back, reliable as a brick wall, no fancy stuff. Well, Gerry deserved a chance . . . At the end, Froggy beckoned them round him and said to Gerry: "Fair enough, son—you'll be our reserve for the St. Kenelm match, O.K.? You've come on a lot—someone been coaching you? Your dad?"

Gerry shook his head dumbly. He couldn't say "a boy called Phil". He was half delighted, half disappointed. Reserve—it was something, but what if he just stood all through the match, watching the others struggle? That would be worse than not being chosen at all. Still: "Thanks, Fr—Mr. Froggett," he said hastily.

Ginger banged him on the back. "Not so dusty, Titch!"

"It'll be a tough match, and we'll have to plan our tactics. Extra practice Saturday morning, to work it out," Froggy told them.

When Gerry rushed home and told his father, he felt better. Mr. Holt's face split into a happy grin. "Well done,

Gerry. You're bound to play—St. Kenelm's always knock the other side about."

"Hope so—hope I don't muck it up," Gerry said, suddenly scared for a new reason.

" 'Course you won't. Your mother and I'll both come, so you'll have your own private supporters' club to keep an eye on you."

"And mind you clean your boots—I'm ashamed to see you playing in that state," his mother said, smiling. She was equally pleased, Gerry saw. It would be great having them both there.

"Did you ever beat the Killers, Dad?" he asked.

"No, son, never. We drew with 'em, I remember, but when we went over there for the return match, they beat us." His father sighed, and his face looked sad. "It was tragic, what happened. We'd worked so hard, especially our centre-forward, and we were all set to wipe the floor with 'em. But it wasn't to be."

"Why, what happened?"

Mr. Holt hesitated. "Tell you after the match," he said at last.

So, as it turned out, Gerry didn't go down to the school again for a solitary practice, and didn't see Phil. There was no time. On Saturday they practised all morning with Froggy, and he was whacked. On Sunday they went over to see his grandmother for the day. Then when Gerry woke on Monday he realised it was the day of the match, and his stomach lurched. It was all happening too fast.

The others pulled his leg all day, but he didn't mind. It was different, now he'd been picked. Even being called Titch didn't rankle.

"Have a sweet, Titch—got to keep your strength up," said Ginger.

"You'll be our secret weapon," said Dave cheerfully. "They'll never see you till you've got the ball away from them!"

"Don't forget your shin-pads," Ginger warned. "They're hackers, all of 'em."

59

After an endless dragging afternoon the bell rang, and St. Kenelm's team rolled up in a coach. They piled out laughing and shouting. "Full of themselves," Ginger said, as they came pouring into the cloakroom to change, swinging their games bags, cheerfully jostling the Fairfield side. "Think they're going to wipe the floor with us."

"They never get beaten, that's the trouble," someone else said with a sigh.

Gerry silently pulled his blue shirt over his head and squatted to tie up his boots. They certainly looked a tough side, close to.

When both teams ran out, there was a trickle of clapping round the field. A lot of the school were there to watch, and some St. Kenelm boys had cycled over and were waving red scarves and shouting. There were a few parents standing on the touchline—Gerry saw his own among them. He was glad they'd come, but he wanted to keep by himself. He didn't want to talk, and his mother might fuss. He ran up one side of the field away from everyone, and waited tensely. Froggy was refereeing—that was one good thing.

The whistle went, and the game began. St. Kenelm's won the toss and were playing down the slope. They charged confidently into action, sweeping the opposition out of the way. They hadn't earned their nickname for nothing! They had brawn on their side, and they used it. Johnny Kent, in goal, was kept frantically busy leaping from one side to the other without let-up. He saved three hard shots, but then a groan went up as a striker shot the ball hard past his clutching fingers. The St. Kenelm supporters chanted their delight. Gerry swallowed, looking at the dejected Fairfield team. It was an awful start.

Suddenly Phil was at his elbow. "Hi," he said.

"Hi." Gerry was delighted. He didn't mind talking to Phil, he was different. "I'm reserve."

Phil nodded, as if he knew already.

"They're good, aren't they," Gerry went on.

Phil shrugged. "They're not as good as they think."

"Probably beat us about five nothing," Gerry said. He was starting secretly to hope he wouldn't have to play.

They stood watching in silence. Dave got the ball and had a long shot, but a defender intercepted. Play ranged up and down the field, Fairfield looking desperate. St. Kenelm's were attacking again, to roars from their supporters. They were up around the goal, threatening. Wham! The ball hit the crossbar and rebounded. But there was no reprieve. A winger drove it in. Two nothing.

The Fairfield team looked wanly at each other. So far they hadn't had one real chance, and they didn't know what to do. Gerry glumly wondered what his dad was thinking.

"We want three! We want three!" Gerry heard the St. Kenelm's boys shouting joyously, and he clenched his fists and hated them.

"What do you think?" he said to Phil.

"They haven't won yet," Phil answered shortly. He seemed to hate St. Kenelm's just as much.

Half-time came and went. Froggy must have forgotten all about him—Gerry couldn't decide if he was relieved or not. Then the whistle went. Gerry craned forward. Dave was on the ground, clutching at his ankle. Froggy ran up, had a look at him, then sent him off. Ah—yes, he was beckoning Gerry on! Gerry was petrified, his legs wouldn't move.

"You'll be all right. Go on," Phil said. His quiet voice calmed the other boy's nerves. Swallowing, Gerry jogged on to the pitch.

"Do your best, Titch," Dave said, hobbling past him. "I've twisted my ankle, darn it. Wish one of *them* would!"

There was not a second to feel nervous out there. Gerry was in the thick of it at once. He got the ball, was charged hard, but hung on. St. Kenelm's were all around him, red shirts everywhere. Desperately he passed to Ginger, who got away and tore down the field, the defenders in hot pursuit. Ginger, unable to see the goal for a forest of legs, shot at random. A wild, unbelieving cheer went up.

He'd scored! It was a fluke, but it counted. Fairfield felt better.

"That's more like it," said Mr. Holt with satisfaction.

"I do hope Gerry doesn't get hurt," said his wife anxiously. "He looks so small out there compared with all the others."

"Don't you worry about him, he's as good as any of 'em," said Gerry's dad proudly.

The game rushed on, tough, no holds barred. There wasn't much time left. Gerry was marked closely, but kept trying. Suddenly the ball came bouncing to his feet. He got it and took off down the field. A defender loomed up, and Gerry passed to Ginger and ran on. Ginger, surrounded, shot it back high towards him. Now what? Gerry panicked, seeing the ball descending from the sky. Suddenly Phil was there beside him, though nobody else seemed to notice. He was there, urgently shouting into Gerry's ear: "Go on, head it, head it!" Taking a deep breath, Gerry jumped and headed it, taking it just right, miraculously, twisting it diagonally towards the goal. It was going like a bullet, and it twisted into the corner of the net. The St. Kenelm goalie didn't have a chance.

"Well done, Titch!" Ginger and a couple of others were banging him hard on the back, crowding round him, pummelling him. "Good for you—great stuff!"

Gerry couldn't believe it. It was wonderful and satisfying, and he wouldn't have swopped places with a star in the First Division at that moment. But he couldn't understand why no one had shouted at Phil to get off the pitch. You'd think Froggy would have gone for him, and disallowed the goal, even. Talk about against the rules . . .

St. Kenelm's were looking sick, and no wonder. They couldn't understand what was going wrong. They'd expected the match to be a pushover. Their supporters, too, had gone quiet, staring uneasily. St. Kenelm's had, in fact, been cut down to size, and no longer did they look unbeatable. Gerry's goal had taken the heart out of them.

Fairfield were suddenly happy. Things were flowing their

Phil shot ferociously . . .

way, and their confidence came surging back. Two totally unexpected goals had done wonders for them. "Come on— just time for one more!" Ginger was shouting as soon as they started again, and they all charged eagerly down the pitch.

There was a scrimmage all around the goal, defenders and attackers muddled up together. St. Kenelm's desperately tried to form a wall, shouting conflicting instructions to each other. Gerry, panting, struggled to hang on to the ball. A tall St. Kenelm's defender knocked him down hard, jolting him painfully on the ground, then lashed out at the ball to clear it. The chance had gone! But then Phil was there, on to the ball like lighting, moving faster than Gerry had ever seen anyone move before. "No, Phil, get off—you mustn't!" Gerry gasped. But without pausing Phil shot ferociously, and the ball zoomed inside the net. He spun round towards Gerry then, and for the first time Gerry saw his teeth flashing in an overjoyed, conspiratorial grin. Then he was gone—totally gone, not a sign of him.

"A great own goal!" Ginger shouted in Gerry's ear.

Gerry stared at him, then at the St. Kenelm defender, who was drooping his head. An own goal? But Phil had scored it—hadn't he? His head spun.

Anyhow, it was three-two when the final whistle went, a few minutes later. St. Kenelm's trailed off, bewildered and numb. They'd had the heart knocked out of them. Fairfield came in with their arms round each other, tired but triumphant. They could hardly believe it, but it had happened. Somehow they'd beaten the team who never lost. Froggy thumped them all on the back. "Well done, lads! Great game!"

When Gerry came wearily out of school a few minutes later, he found his father waiting. Mr. Holt said warmly: "I'm proud of you, old son. You all played great stuff." He added thoughtfully: "That goal of yours reminded me of how Phil Gaskell used to score. He headed 'em in just like that."

"Phil Gaskell?" Gerry echoed.

"Yes, he was our centre-forward, the best of us all. Lived for football—a lonely kid he was, nobody knew much about him, and he never talked much, but he was magic on the field. He was killed cycling to St. Kenelm's when we were due to play them in that match I told you about, years ago. Tore across the road in front of a lorry. Tragic, it was. I think he couldn't wait to get at 'em."

Gerry felt as if somebody had punched him in the stomach, knocking all the breath out of him. Silently he walked on.

Next morning before assembly he stole into the hall. He'd been trying to work it all out ever since he woke up. He studied the old football groups closely until at last he found the right one. It was dated twenty-six years ago. There sat Phil in the middle of the group, clasping the ball. Even in the faded photo his freckles showed up, and his shorts were the same baggy ones. Gerry stood staring, a strange tingling down his back. At last, he said under his breath: "We'd never have done it without you. Thanks, Phil."

STELLA

by ROSEMARY TIMPERLEY

ROBERT was used to the Underground journey between home and school. At first he had been rather nervous in the tube train, aware of a shut-in feeling, conscious of the weight of earth above his head; but custom had dulled such irrational fears and now, when he could get a seat, he settled down quite happily to read or catch up on home-work which should have been done the night before.

On this particular morning, however, he felt jumpy. The roar of the train and darkness of the tunnels seemed sinister. He had that something-is-going-to-happen sensa-tion and couldn't concentrate on the chapter in his history text-book which he was trying to absorb.

He glanced at his fellow-passengers. A girl sitting oppo-site him caught his eye, leaned forward and asked softly: "Are you feeling all right?" She had a soft, Irish voice, musical.

"Yes," said Robert, feeling foolish. "Why?"

"You've gone so pale. I thought maybe you felt sick."

"No, I—I can't get this wretched history into my head, that's all, and we've got an exam this morning."

"Poor old you," said the girl. "That's enough to make anyone feel like death. I remember the state I got into when I took my nursing exams. Nervous! I was as tense as a fiddle-string."

"Did you pass the exams?" Robert asked.

"I did."

"So you're a nurse now."

"That's right. I'm just on my way to the hospital."

"Do you like nursing?"

"I like the work very much, but it's terribly tiring. Sometimes I feel too exhausted to go on." She was awfully thin, he thought, and she had dark shadows under her eyes.

"You're on your feet all the time, aren't you?" he said.

"That's the physical side of it, but it's emotionally wearing, too. I suppose I care too much about the patients. I've always cared too much about every suffering thing. It's as if I enter into their feelings, and it takes it out of you. A doctor has warned me that I may have to give it up, and then I don't know what I shall do with myself."

"Oh, what a shame!" said Robert, for she looked so sad. "Well, I think you're very brave to——"

He never completed his sentence, for there was a sudden tremendous noise: an explosion which seemed to pierce the ear-drums and deaden the brain. The lights went out. People screamed. There was a sound of glass breaking. Robert felt a stab of pain in his head. The screams around him turned weird, unearthly. Then they faded and all was silent darkness . . . His last thought was: I'm dying. So this is how it feels . . .

Later, he didn't know how much later, Robert opened his eyes. So he hadn't died after all. He was still in the Underground carriage and the girl who'd said she was a nurse was still there. The other passengers had gone and the train was rattling along as if nothing had occurred.

"What was that awful bang?" Robert asked dazedly.

"I don't know," the girl answered.

"I must have fainted or something," said Robert. "I didn't even see the other passengers get out."

"Nor did I," said the girl, and laughed. "Anyway, we've got the carriage to ourselves now, which is rather nice." She seemed more lively than before and quite unperturbed, but Robert was desperately uneasy. He had never known the morning train to empty out like this. Was it possible that the others had been told to get out, and he and the girl hadn't heard because they were unconscious and no one had bothered about them?

"I thought I heard the windows breaking, too," he said, "but they aren't even cracked. Anyway, the lights are on again——" He stopped. He was staring at the colour of the seats. Instead of being brownish with a dark pattern, they were plain green. A very fresh, lovely green. Like new grass. But he was in no mood to be consoled by a pretty colour.

"We're in a different train!" he cried.

The girl looked round. "So we are. A better one, too."

"Never mind about better—where's it taking us?"

They looked out of the windows but there was only the blackness of tunnel walls to be seen.

"Don't worry. We'll know where we are when we reach a station," said the girl. The stations on the line were not very far apart and they should reach the next one at any moment.

Except that they didn't. The train went on and on, into the dark, as if this were a line without stations.

"It's not only a different train, it's a different line," Robert pointed out.

"Then when we get to the end of the line, you can go back," the girl said soothingly. "Relax, my dear. When there's nothing you can do about a situation, accept it and conserve your strength. Don't get worked up."

"My head hurts!"

"Yes. Let me try to make it better. Look, there's a green carpet on the floor. It's a lovely train. You lie on the floor, and I'll sit down and lean against a seat, then you can put your head in my lap. Let's pretend you're one of my patients and I'm going to look after you till you're well again."

Robert felt so rotten that he obeyed her. Soon he was lying on the green carpet, his head in her lap, and he felt her hands on his forehead. He couldn't tell what she was doing, but the pain receded.

"Thank you," he said. "It's not throbbing so badly now. Are *you* feeling all right?"

"Me? I feel marvellous. All my tiredness has gone."

"Aren't you frightened? We don't know where we're going."

"No one ever really knows where he is going," she said. "People think they do sometimes, but they're usually wrong."

"What's your name?" he asked her now.

"Stella. And yours?"

"Robert. That's pretty—'Stella'. It means 'star', doesn't it?" He looked up into her face as she smiled down at him. "You're a super nurse, Stella, and you're shining like a star. There's a sort of glow around you. Like an angel in a picture. Do you know, Stella, I think this must be a dream."

"No, because we're both in it."

"Maybe we're not—maybe you're part of my dream."

"Well! Talk about the arrogance of the male."

"Sorry." Robert chuckled and Stella laughed outright.

"Neither of us is dreaming," she said. "This is real and happening. The difference between us is that I accept without question and you're still struggling because your questions aren't answered."

"I wish we could reach a station, that's all," he sighed —and suddenly the train burst out of the tunnel and into the open. The scenery around them was breathtaking.

Purple mountains rose on either side of the track. Silver waterfalls glittered in bright sunshine. Emerald green fields lay at the foot of the hills. Birds were singing.

The train stopped against a green bank. The doors opened.

Robert forgot all about his headache and sprang to his feet.

"Oh, how beautiful!" he said. "I don't care where we are. I'm glad we came. Let's get out and walk right across the fields, and climb the tallest mountain——" He turned to Stella. She had gone.

Then he saw that she had already alighted from the train and was moving swiftly over the grass. "Hey, wait for me!" he called. She turned and waved, but didn't wait.

He rushed to the nearest door—but already it was beginning to close, in that inexorable way that tube train doors do close. He struggled to hold it open, but it was useless. He was trapped again. The train was already beginning to move back towards the tunnel, back into the dark . . .

He beat his fists against the glass. "Stella! Stella!" he cried. "Oh, Stella . . ."

"This one's coming round," said a voice. "A near thing. I thought he was a gonner when we found him."

"You ambulance men are so pessimistic," said a woman's voice.

And Robert found himself lying on a trolley with a red blanket draped over him. A woman in a nurse's cap was looking down at him. A nurse—but not *his* nurse. "Where's Stella gone?" he asked.

"Who's Stella? A friend you were travelling with?"

"Yes. She got out at the end of the line—she was going towards the hills—it was so beautiful——"

A man in a white coat replaced the nurse. "Let's have a look at that head. Hello, old boy. Lie still. I'm a doctor." Hands on his head. Gentle. But not like Stella's hands. "Mmm. Not as bad as it might be. I wonder what stopped the bleeding."

"Stella did, I expect," said Robert. "She said she'd make it better."

But the doctor wasn't listening. "Wheel him along to X-ray, please, Nurse. Now, who's next?"

The trolley moved. Robert lay staring at a series of different ceilings. And after that it was all go: X-ray room, being heaved on and off a couch, back on the trolley, operating theatre, the doctor again, an injection in his head so the wound could be sewn up without his feeling pain, conversation between the doctor and two nurses, all very casual—running down hospital food mostly: "The staff canteen gets worse and worse," and so on. Then there was another trolley-ride and he was put to bed in a ward, given a white tablet with a glass of water, and told to lie down and sleep. The white pill filled his head with fluffy white clouds. Robert slept.

He dreamed of the purple mountains at the end of the line. He dreamed that he saw Stella; tireless, happy, glowing, climbing the highest mountain, getting right to the top, and then stretching out her arms towards the sun and the sky—and taking off—like a bird in flight—soaring and singing—a white bird making a journey to a star—but she *was* a star—Stella——

He woke up. "Stella——"

"It's me, darling." His mother was there.

"Oh, Mum!" Arms around him. Tears on his cheeks. His mother's tears. He'd never seen her cry before. "Don't cry, I'm all right," he said. "Stella made me all right first, then the doctor sewed me up. I'm fine. And we went on the strangest journey. Through miles of dark tunnels, then into the open, and the mountains——"

"You've been dreaming," said his mother.

"Just now, I have, but before then, I wasn't. I didn't dream what happened in the train. You ask Stella, when she comes back."

"Darling, who is this Stella you keep talking about?"

"A nurse I met on the train. We stayed together after the big bang. Oh—what *was* that bang? What hit me on the head?"

"Time for another little pill," said a voice in uniform.

And his mother gave him a kiss and went away. He slept again.

Next day he was allowed to go home as long as he promised to take things easy. Only then did he find out, from his mother, what had happened in the train. Some maniac had planted a small bomb in the carriage. When it went off, there were moments of chaos. People had been injured by falling objects and flying glass. The train had stopped, officials had made their way to the damaged carriage and, as the explosion had occurred near a station, those who had only minor injuries had been able to walk the little way along the line and be taken straight to hospital.

Robert had been knocked unconscious by something falling on his head, so he had been carried out by ambulance men.

"Quite a mercy that you were knocked out, really, darling," said his mother, "for the next thing you knew, after the big bang, was that you were safe in hospital, being looked after."

"But Stella looked after me first," said Robert, "and we went to the end of the line together—a different line— a different train."

"No, Robert. That was a dream you had when you were unconscious."

"It wasn't a dream," he insisted, "because Stella and I were both in it. She pointed that out to me. People don't have the same dream together. It's impossible. If a thing happens to two people at once, it's really happening. Stella went for a walk in the countryside at the end of the line. She'll have caught a train back by now, whatever that train was. I *did* have a dream in which she turned into a bird and flew away from the top of the mountain— that *was* a dream—and I knew it when I woke up. It was quite different from the real part."

"All right, darling," said his mother. "Forget about it now, anyway. It's over."

"Forget it? I'll never forget Stella! I'm going to find her again. I know her first name, and she's a nurse, so I'll be able to get in touch with her if I try. She was so tired and sad before the big bang, but afterwards she was lively and happy and—Oh, I loved her! And she looked after me. She may even have saved my life. The doctor wondered what had stopped the bleeding when he first examined me. Well, Stella did that."

His mother said nothing. She was looking evasive, half-guilty.

"You're keeping something from me," said Robert.

"No——"

"You are. What is it? Mum—did—did anyone die in the train?"

"Yes. One person. Oh, all right, Robert, I'll tell you. When the ambulance men picked you up, you were lying on the floor with your head in a girl's lap. And—darling, you mustn't let this upset you—but the girl was dead. She'd been killed outright in the explosion. Her name was Stella O'Brien. She was a nurse."

Robert stared ahead of him, speechless. His mother brought him a newspaper. "There's a full account of the incident here. Read it for yourself, love. Sorry I tried to hide it. Not very honest of me."

"That's all right," Robert murmured, and he read the paper.

What his mother had said was true.

"I know what happened now," he told her. "I must have almost died, too. I went part of the way with her. Then she got out at the end of the line, but I came back. She *said* I'd be going back. She knew. It's true," he insisted. "Otherwise how could I possibly have known her name? She didn't tell me until long after the big bang that her name was Stella."

He swallowed tears. "I mustn't cry," he said. "She wasn't happy here—her work was too much for her. But she's happy now."

" 'Whom the gods love, die young,' " his mother said unexpectedly.

"Yes," said Robert, and smiled.

THIS BOOK BELONGS TO ...

by DAPHNE FROOME

"ISN'T it a really splendid house?" said Jenny's grandfather proudly as he conducted her along the wide gravel path to the front door.

Jenny, instead of replying, gazed doubtfully at the large, rather tumbledown building with its untidy collection of added rooms, fussily arched windows, twisted wrought-iron balconies, and groups of chimneys leaning dangerously over the sagging slate roof. The whole effect was made even more grotesque by two incongruous turreted towers with battlements.

"It was built in the eighteen-thirties," her grandfather continued. "We're really quite proud of the place. The architecture's mock Gothic. There are any number of useful out-buildings, and sheds at the back as well, and a honeycomb of cellars underground. We haven't had time to explore those yet, but you can get a glimpse of them before going indoors by looking down the shute where they used to tip the coal."

Jenny followed him round the side of the house and watched while he lifted a manhole cover near one of the walls and revealed a large, damp, cobwebby cavity, disappearing into nothingness. Nodding without enthusiasm, she hoped that the exploration of the cellars would be left until after she had finished her holiday and returned home.

Her grandmother greeted her in the hall and led her upstairs and along a twisting corridor to a room at the end of the house.

"I've put you here because it has a lovely view out of both of the windows," she said. "You can see the river in one direction and look out over the old farm buildings in the other. I wish the room under this one was the sitting-room, and not the library, as the present sitting-room only faces the road—but the built-in bookcases would be very difficult to move."

Jenny felt obliged to admire the size of the rooms and their curious shapes.

"I never thought we'd be able to afford a grand home like this," her grandmother admitted, "but it's so dilapidated we were able to buy it very cheaply. The last owner went abroad many years ago and after some while decided not to come back here, so it's been left empty for ages. That's why it's so neglected. It'll be very pleasant, though, when we've got it nicely furnished." She paused. "We're very glad to see you, but I'm afraid you won't have much of a holiday this time."

"That's all right," Jenny replied. "It'll be interesting helping you move in."

It was rather like camping at first, Jenny decided, because the cooker hadn't arrived, and they had to manage on a couple of primus stoves, and necessary things like the tin-opener and the iron seemed to have been mislaid during the move; but the old house, with its twisting corridors and large overgrown garden (which, her grandfather said optimistically, would be marvellous once the weeds had been dealt with) proved far more fascinating than Jenny had first thought it would be, and she was quite happy helping her grandparents to arrange their furniture and hang up curtains.

One day, Jenny went into the library and found her grandfather standing at the top of a pair of very tall steps.

"I'm cleaning the shelves," he said, "getting ready to arrange all my books. They'll look good here, won't they."

The top shelves were so high that they almost touched the ceiling, with its decoration of fat plaster cherubs that always made Jenny want to laugh. She ran to steady the steps, which had begun to sway dangerously as her grandfather suddenly stood on tiptoe and, scrabbling about in one corner, retrieved a dust-covered book.

He gave it to Jenny and climbed down the steps to the floor.

Jenny blew off the dust, sneezed, and read out: " 'The Knights of Hampden Castle,' by Richard Carter." Then she opened the book. Inside, on the endpaper, was a bookplate inscribed in rather flowery writing with the name Mabel Anne, and the date: 1839.

"I wish she'd written her surname," grumbled Jenny.

"Some people are never satisfied," her grandfather answered crustily. "I wonder if it's a good story."

Jenny handed him the book, and he glanced quickly down the first few pages. "Travel, adventure, brave knights, treasure—it looks like a marvellous yarn to me, a cross between 'Ivanhoe' and 'Robinson Crusoe' with a bit of 'Treasure Island' added for good measure. Though 'Treasure Island' was written much later than this, of course. Well, I can't stand here reading all day," he said as he handed the book back to Jenny. "I've work to do."

"It is a beautiful book," Jenny remarked, "but the edges of the paper are very uneven. And look—those at the end are still fastened together."

"Books are printed in sheets," her grandfather explained, "each of which contains quite a few pages. Then the sheets are folded into sections, and gathered together carefully in the right order and sewn up. So when the book is first put together many of the pages are still joined to each other at the edges. These days the pages are then cut by machinery, but it was not always so. Mabel Anne obviously had to get these cut by hand. By the look of the uneven way they've been separated she probably did it herself." He grunted. "You children don't realize how much is done for you these days."

Jenny hardly heard him. She was far too immersed in reading the first page of the book, then the second. This was no ordinary story—it gripped her from the very beginning, and went on to become more and more exciting with every enthralling line. She trundled a large leather arm-chair across to the window and, snuggling into it, began reading and reading . . .

Jenny's grandfather finished cleaning the shelves, then he folded the steps and put them away in a corner. "I'm going to have some tea now," he said, but Jenny neither heard him nor noticed when he went away.

Outside in the garden, the bright bare silhouettes of the winter trees gradually lost their sharpness as they began to merge into the darkening sky.

Jenny screwed up her eyes to try to focus on the print better. She thought she heard a faint sound in the room and looked round, expecting to see a grown-up about to say to her, as they so often did: "You'll ruin your eyes, reading in a bad light like that." But there was no one there. It was very cold and she thought that she had been foolish to sit there so long.

There seemed to be a draught blowing from somewhere behind her.

"Bother," she said, and went over and closed the door. "These old houses," she grumbled as she settled down again, and suddenly she wished she was back home with her parents in their small, comfortable flat.

The draught seemed to be stronger than ever. She looked round, wondering where it could possibly be coming from, and as she did so it caught the pages of the book, and flicked them over.

"Bother," said Jenny again. "Now I've lost my place. Oh, I'll go somewhere else."

She closed the book and stood up, but the draught caught at her hair, sending it across her eyes so that she blundered into the shelves, and at that moment the book was snatched from her hand and flung to the floor.

Instantly the draught died away. Jenny stared around her, and then, leaving the book where it had fallen, she rushed from the room in a panic.

"A haunted library!" exclaimed her grandfather, laughing. "I hardly think *that's* very likely. The library certainly *is* a draughty room—I must get something done about it— or else perhaps the book was so exciting it gave you the shivers."

"Well, it *is* exciting," replied Jenny grudgingly.

"Yes, I dare say," replied her grandfather. Then he changed the subject. "Your grandmother's tired, she's been shopping all day, so how about coming down to earth and giving her a hand with the supper?"

As the days of her visit went by without further incident, Jenny, who had not dared to venture into the library again, began to believe that perhaps after all she *had* only imagined the haunting. "It was all the effect of reading that exciting story on a gloomy winter's day," she decided.

Passing the library door one afternoon, she peered rather diffidently in. The room seemed perfectly ordinary; in fact it looked quite inviting with the winter sun streaming through the glass, picking out the gold letters and colourful spines of the books her grandfather had arranged on the shelves, the beautiful soft shades of the carpet he had laid, and the shiny surface of the round beaten brass table that her grandmother had spent so long cleaning up. Her grandfather had left his newspaper and reading glasses on the table and she noticed that he had hung his valuable collection of eighteenth-century prints over the fireplace. Obviously he didn't believe the room was haunted. She could quite distinctly see the exciting book, put back on one of the shelves.

Walking into the room, she took down the book, sat in the armchair and began to read where she had left off before. She had been reading for some time when a small, polite, but quite unmistakable cough made her jump.

A strange girl was standing in a corner of the room, her face in deep shadow, but Jenny could see that her long, dark hair was parted in the middle and tied back from her face with two neat ribbon bows, and she was so thin that

78

her elaborate, high-necked, velvet dress, with its full skirt and white frilly apron, hung about her in deep folds.

Silently the girl began to move across the room. As she advanced into the fading light her shadowy figure became if anything less distinct.

The apparition wavered, then disappeared, only to appear once more, bending over the chair in which Jenny was sitting.

Jenny, shrinking back as far as she was able, caught a brief glimpse of a pair of wistful blue eyes as the girl gazed into her face before glancing downwards to the book. Then the figure turned away and was gone.

"A ghost!" exclaimed Jenny's grandfather. "You just imagined it, sitting there thinking about the girl who owned the book."

"I'm sure it *was* Mabel Anne," Jenny insisted, and she began to shiver violently.

"The child's had a shock; she'd be better off in bed," said Jenny's grandmother, and she hustled Jenny upstairs and insisted on tucking her in beneath a couple of extra blankets.

"You must keep warm, dear," she added. "I'd never forgive myself if you fell ill. Don't worry now. I was always imagining things when I was your age."

Jenny, left alone, dozed uncomfortably beneath the extra weight of the bedclothes, disturbed by strange dreams of Mabel Anne bending over her. They were very upsetting dreams, and she was glad when her grandmother woke her.

"I'm just on my way to bed," she explained. "I've brought you a hot drink and that book you were so interested in. If you find difficulty in getting back to sleep again you may like to read for a bit."

Jenny, propped up among the pillows, sipping the warm drink, felt slightly comforted. After all, the ghost—if there was one—lived in the library, not here in her bedroom. She took up the book and slowly turned the pages until she came to the place where she had left off reading before.

It was certainly by far the most gripping tale she had ever come across, and, forgetting everything in the excitement of the story, she read on and on until she was almost at the end. Then, suddenly——

"Bother!" she exclaimed as she found she could not turn over the next page. She had come to the last section, where the edges still needed cutting.

She climbed out of bed and hunted in the pockets of her jeans until she found her penknife. Then she placed the book on her bedside table and began very carefully to separate the edges of the pages. It was a far more difficult task than she would have supposed, because the table was ricketty and the pages were made of very thick paper.

Once she was sure she heard a sound from the library below. She paused, listening anxiously, but the house was silent again. She must have been mistaken, she decided.

After quite a struggle she completed her task and was just climbing back into bed, holding the book, when she heard the library door rattle. There was a pause of a few seconds of complete silence, then the lampshade began to sway as a soft draught blew under the door. Jenny shivered, then sat rigid, clutching the book even tighter in her nervousness. Mabel Anne was slowly materializing. There was an anxious, almost yearning expression in her thin, pinched face.

The ghost glided, shimmering, across the room, and as Jenny drew back, fearful of being enveloped completely, she settled beside her on the bed and stared fixedly at the book. Shakily, Jenny thrust it towards her, then cringed as a strong current of air flung open the cover and ruffled the pages, turning them a dozen or so at a time. Jenny suddenly realised that the ghost of Mabel Anne barely possessed the skill to turn the pages individually, and certainly not to cut them. She looked so terribly ill. Perhaps she had died before finishing the story, and her poor ghost had hung around ever since, waiting to know how it ended.

Mabel Anne was quite unable to control the newly-cut

The girl stared fixedly at the book . . .

pages, which were sticking together and turning over two at a time as the cold draught whipped them this way and that. Jenny cautiously put out her hand and steadied the book, then found her place again. Though her fingers were numb and frozen she managed to turn the pages, scanning the lines and trying to gauge the speed of the other girl's reading, but the ghost flickered impatiently long before Jenny finished each one. She decided Mabel Anne must be a much quicker reader than she was.

Eventually the last page was completed and the book closed. Then Mabel Anne seemed to drift away, turning towards her and bowing her head regally in thanks, and Jenny found herself staring at nothing more interesting than the faded wallpaper beside her bed.

She replaced the book on the table, pulled the bed-clothes closely around her and tried unsuccessfully to go to sleep.

"You still look terribly tired," her grandmother said the next day.

"I stayed up late finishing that book," Jenny replied.

"Was it good?"

"Oh, yes. I've never read anything better."

"You can take it home if you like, as you seem to think it's so marvellous."

"No, thank you," Jenny answered very firmly. "I think it should be left here in the bookcase, where it belongs."

A GHOST IN THE FAMILY

by CHRISTINE PULLEIN-THOMPSON

I DIDN'T want to be riding for ever wtth the Nelsons because I like riding alone, writing poetry in my head and singing my favourite songs with no one to laugh at my monotonous, tuneless voice. But they kept ringing up.

We were new to the district. Dad is a doctor and had become Registrar at the local hospital, and Mum had found herself a job at the library. At fifteen, I was a gangling, brown-haired beanpole of five foot six. Dad said the Nelsons must think I was lonely, and Mum, who has a romantic mind, said they wanted an escort for their three daughters.

I had two ponies, then, grey Nimrod and black Jack Daw. Jack Daw was my favourite, though he had appalling manners. I think I preferred him because he was a challenge to ride and he was black. I have always loved black horses, and because of this I plan to join the Household Cavalry when I leave school.

The Nelsons were a strange family. There were five children, three girls and two boys, and they lived in a house called Dark Dingle. They rode quite differently from me, galloping over stones, along verges, leaping stiles, their ponies' manes unbrushed, their crash caps pushed low over their eyes. But one couldn't help liking them, for they were always full of ideas and for ever running things—from jumble sales and fêtes to gymkhanas. Locally they were known as "them young devils from the Dingle", and they had a reputation for supreme recklessness.

I liked Carl and Melanie best. Carl had a wild face which made you think of gipsies, but he was immensely generous and would lend you the last penny he had.

Melanie was musical in a disorderly way. She was always singing and could play the guitar. George and the twins, Jenny and Debby, were more ordinary. They wore less peculiar clothes and talked about books. The Nelsons had only three ponies between them and were always hinting that Nimrod needed exercising, but I explained that Jack Daw's legs were dicey and I needed a second horse. In this way, I kept them at bay.

We had ridden several times together when Carl suggested that we hacked up to Hangman's Crossroads one night and looked for ghosts. I was in their kitchen at the time, drinking coffee, while Jack Daw stood tied up in the yard.

"Ghosts! You must be mad," I said. "Or do they swing from a gibbet in the dark?"

Melanie smiled. "But they do exist, don't they Carl? Though they don't exactly swing . . ." she said.

It was nearly the end of November. The trees were almost bare of leaves now, and there was an uneasy wind which seemed to tell of storms to come.

"We're serious," said Carl. "Will you come tonight, Francis? Or are you chicken?"

"Dad isn't keen on me riding in the dark," I answered.

"We can lend you a stirrup light—tell him that," replied Melanie.

"I don't see the point," I said. "Why ride in the dark at all?"

"To see the ghosts," said Melanie.

"Have you seen them?" I asked.

"Yes, of course. Lots of people have."

"Actually, it's our great-great-grandfather being murdered. That's what makes it so interesting for us," said Melanie.

"Oh yeah, tell me another," I said scornfully.

"It's true," replied Carl. "Now, are you coming? Or are you scared? We go every year and we don't ask *anyone* to come with us. It really *is* a compliment."

"I'll come, but I don't believe in ghosts and I think you're both mad," I answered.

"It's an awful experience," said Carl. "And if I could get my hands on the murderer. I would tear him to bits . . ."

"Very funny," I said.

"It sends my blood pressure up to breaking point—and your father's a doctor, so you know what that means," Carl added.

"You're talking drivel, but I'll come anyway," I said.

When I reached home, Dad was hanging pictures. I had seen them all before. They were what you call family portraits: aunts and great-aunts, great-uncles and great-great-uncles, grandfathers and great-grandfathers. Some were on horses, but mostly they sat on sofas with their hands folded in their laps, or stood, with strange-looking dogs lying at their feet.

Fortunately, my parents had been invited to a party, so I didn't have to tell them I would be going out in the dark. Presently they left, dressed in clothes suitable for cocktails. I cooked myself sausages and baked beans in our rather stately kitchen, which belongs to an earlier age when there were cooks and scullery maids, and a butler in the pantry. The house is far too large for us, but it was much cheaper than more convenient homes, which is why Dad bought it.

I decided to take Nimrod because, being grey, he would show up better in the dark than Jack Daw. He bit me as I tightened his girths and obviously thought it outside pony rules to be taken out so late at night.

It was a particularly dreary November evening, with drizzle falling like dew. I like riding in the dark; it has no fears for me. I imagine I am a Cavalier fleeing from the Roundheads, or a doctor riding to see a dying patient. But Nimrod was not too keen, and left our old-fashioned stableyard reluctantly.

The road to the Nelsons was straight and empty. They were waiting for me at the end of their drive, Carl riding cobby Choirboy, who looked more like an old man than a boy. Melanie was on roan, Roman-nosed Stepmother, and George rode his big bay, High Court Judge, known simply as Judge. I have never understood why they always chose such long-winded names for their horses.

"So you've come," observed Carl.

"Of course I've come," I said.

"Fantastic!" cried Melanie.

We had no lights between us, not even a torch. I wondered what my father would say if he saw us. He deals with road accidents at the hospital and is always lecturing me on road safety and how carelessness costs lives. So, as we rode towards Hangman's Cross, I prayed the cocktail party would last a long time.

There is a long hill up to Hangman's Cross.

"Don't you want to know a little more about the ghosts?" asked Melanie as cars hooted and dipped their lights at us.

"No, we'll be ghosts ourselves soon enough," I replied. "And I thought you were bringing stirrup lights."

"Don't be such a fusspot," said Carl. "How can man die better than on the back of a horse?"

"Not at fifteen," I answered.

"We must hurry," said Melanie, looking at her watch. "It's due at eight . . ."

"What is?" I asked.

"The stage-coach. He stops it at the top of the hill, the swine. They always did that, because the horses were out of breath then and incapable of galloping away."

"What horses?"

"The ones pulling the stage-coach, of course."

"It's the night coach," added Carl. "So they've put the lame and the blind to pull it. They will have left the Coaching Inn at Hellborough half an hour ago."

"And our great-great-grandfather is in the box," said Melanie.

"The stage-coach drivers were like pop stars then," explained Carl. "Some of them accepted bribes from highwaymen, but our great-great-grandfather never did, and that's why he was shot."

"He was only forty, but then they didn't live long in those days. They drank too much. They had to, or they would have frozen to death on the box," Melanie said.

"They were a special breed of men . . ." continued Carl.

"You seem to have made quite a study of them," I observed.

"Wouldn't you, if your great-great-grandfather had been murdered by a criminal just three miles from where you lived?" asked Carl.

"And can't rest in peace even a hundred and ten years later . . ." added Melanie.

"Who was the highwayman?" I asked.

"History doesn't tell. I think he was caught and hung. I hope so, but no one is sure. We don't know his name, but he had a cultured voice, the stinking rat . . ." said Carl.

We were nearly at the top of the hill now. Nimrod was sweating. There was a thick mist. "Not many cars come this way now," said George. "Not since they built the motorway."

George was thickset. He rode with his legs forward and seat well back in the saddle. His riding set my teeth on edge, if you know what that means. I wanted to say: "Why don't you consider poor old Judge? You wouldn't like to carry a great lump on your back; you would want it near your shoulders, like a knapsack. It's much easier there." But I didn't.

There was nothing at Hangman's Cross except a sign-post and a few trees. The wind whispered in our ears, and far below we could see lights from cottages and smaller, moving lights, flickering like glow-worms along hedge-fenced roads . . .

"It's fantastic at night up here, isn't it? Don't you agree, Francis?" asked Melanie.

"Eerie," I answered. "Like the top of the world. Listen . . . I can hear sheep. What's the time? The cocktail party ends at eight. If Dad sees me here, there will be one heck of a row."

"Three minutes to," said Melanie. "We had better get off the road. Not that side. The highwayman hides behind those trees."

"Of course, they may not come, but it's the right day and the right time," said Carl. "Eight o'clock was quite late then ..."

The horses stood very still, close together, their ears pricked. The wind continued whispering. The drizzle had stopped.

"Gosh, it's quiet," said George.

"Listen, I hear hooves," Melanie said quietly. "They're down in the valley. Listen."

"It's coming, then," said Carl.

There seemed to be something moving on the far side of the road, behind a clump of trees. There was a muffled neigh and the click of a gun. Nimrod broke into a sweat. None of us spoke. We could hear hooves distinctly now, coming steadily, *clip clop, clip clop* ...

There was the rattle of iron wheels. My heart was thumping against my ribs now, and the atmosphere was extraordinary—everything seemed to be waiting, waiting...

All at once, four horses came into sight, their heads down, their nostrils sending up clouds of steam, their breathing laboured.

"Stop!" shouted a voice. "Everyone get out."

A man sat astride a black mare, easily, alone. And the driver on the box, swathed to his ears in a great cape, shouted: "No, not this time, you devil! I would rather die!" He reached inside his cape for a gun, and then there was a single shot and he fell from the box and lay quite still on the road, while the horses stood panting, their coats wet with sweat ...

And I stared at the highwayman, and I knew him.

"That's the end," said Melanie in a small voice, as though we were in the cinema and had come to the end of a film. "There's never any more."

"I wish I knew what happened next," said Carl.

As I looked at the road again, I saw that it was empty, just as it had been before.

"Well?" asked George. "Do you believe us now, Francis?"

"Yes, of course," I answered, trying to place a face, a long, straight nose beneath a mask, a high forehead under a hat . . . In a minute I would know. I would fix the two pieces together—the face I had seen, and the other face.

"He killed him at point blank range; he didn't give him a chance," said Melanie.

"There were rich pickings on board, jewels galore," said George.

"Cowboys were the same—the survivor was the one who was quickest on the draw," I answered.

"You're not sticking up for the highwayman, are you?" said Melanie. "He's a robber—a robber and a killer."

"I wonder why," I said. The faces were coming together now, my memory was piecing them together; and I knew then that the face was that of my great-great-grandfather in the hall, the one who, they said, loved black horses—just like me. I didn't know what to say. I had heard so much about him; he had been a very rich man when he died, and we still benefited from his wealth. He had owned a pack of hounds and had built a fine house. And yet there was no mistaking him for, in the picture in our hall, he sat astride the same horse—the highwayman's black mare.

"You're very silent," said Melanie, after we had been riding homewards for some time. "What's the matter?"

"I'm thinking," I answered. "It's all very difficult, really, because . . . well, that man on the black horse . . . I believe he was my great-great-grandfather."

"He can't be!" replied Carl after a short, shocked silence. "I told you—no one knows who he was . . ."

"His picture hangs in our hall. Come and see it tomorrow," I suggested. "It's the truth. I wish it wasn't . . ."

After a pause, Melanie said, in a voice tight with emotion: "We can't know you now. We can't ever speak to you again. Our great-great-grandfather was a wonderful man. He could drive a team of four anywhere. He was the most famous stage-coach driver of his time."

"No wonder you are so well off," said George with a short laugh. "Have you still got any of the jewels he stole?"

"I think we have. Goodnight," I answered.

I trotted away from them, suddenly wishing that I had never spoken. Nimrod was glad to be going home. Cars hooted at us. One driver wound his window down to shout: "Where are your bl . . . . y lights?"

My father was waiting for me, grim-faced, in our big hall.

"What the devil have you been doing?" he shouted.

Mum said: "We've been scared. We were about to ring the police. What's the matter? You look as though you've seen a ghost."

"I have—several . . ." I told them. It all seemed impossible now, and yet I knew it was true. I turned to stare at the portrait of the man who had been my great-great-grandfather on my father's side, and it was the same man on the same horse, only now he was dressed like a rich gentleman . . . I wanted to laugh, but I couldn't.

"He was a highwayman," I said, pointing at the portrait. "I saw him tonight, holding up a coach at the top of Hangman's Hill. Ask the Nelsons. He was murdering their great-great-grandfather. Funny, isn't it? He was just a common robber." I was half crying, half laughing.

"You had better go to bed," said Dad. "You look all in."

"Everything will seem different in the morning," added Mum, as though I were a small, overtired child.

But as I climbed our wide, as yet uncarpeted stairs, I knew it wouldn't. I lay in bed dreading what the Nelsons might do. Supposing they told the whole neighbourhood? I tossed and turned and, since everything always grows worse at night in bed, I imagined Dad losing his job. Mum sacked by the library, and all because I had told the Nelsons the truth.

In the morning, Melanie telephoned. Her voice was small and determined. "We don't want to see the portrait. We believe you," she said. "But, since blood is thicker than water, we have decided that we can never speak to you again. I hope you understand." And with that passing shot she put down the receiver.

"That's that," I said.

Dad was behind me. I relayed what Melanie had just told me.

"But he wasn't your great-great-grandfather," Dad said. "Tell them to come. I can explain everything. You needn't be enemies."

"But you can't explain. He's there!" I cried, pointing. "Even the horse is the same."

"Do as you're told. I've got an hour to spare. Tell them to come at once." Dad picked up the telephone receiver. "Number?" he asked. "What's their number?"

"Two six seven two."

I could hear Melanie answering, then Dad was saying: "Will you come over at once? I want to put the record straight about your great-great-grandfather and the highwayman."

Melanie sounded surprised. There was a short silence before she replied: "O.K., we'll come."

Mum began to clean the hall in a demented manner. "Why do you always ask people when the house is in a mess?" she asked.

"The Nelsons don't notice mess. You should see their house," I said.

Dad unlocked a drawer in his desk and took out an ancient envelope with red sealing wax on it. "Skeletons in the family cupboard," he said. "I never thought I would have to do this. And why did we name you Francis, for heaven's sake? Why not James?"

Rain was falling outside now, washing the last of the leaves from the trees. I ate a bowl of cornflakes in the kitchen without noticing what I was doing and buttered some bread automatically, like a robot.

Five minutes later Carl, Melanie and George arrived on an odd assortment of bicycles.

"That was quick. Come in," said Dad, opening the door and bowing.

"We are eaten up by curiosity," Melanie told him.

"And there he is!" cried Carl, looking at the portrait. "It's unmistakable—even the horse is the same."

"Yes," murmured Melanie, standing behind her brother, while George said: "I don't know why we are here. This place makes me sick."

"Steady there, not so fast," replied Dad in his best bed-side manner. "You mustn't judge without the evidence."

"We've seen that on Hangman's Hill," declared George.

"I'd better tell you our side of the story, then," said Dad. "And in this envelope I have the proof. The man you're looking at on the wall is my great-great-grandfather, Sir James Welberry Sincock; the highwayman you saw was his twin brother, Francis Welberry Sincock, twenty minutes younger and never to have the title, or much money, because of that."

"But the horse?" muttered Melanie.

"He's the same. James acquired him after his brother was hanged. He was particularly fond of black horses. I have all the documents here." Dad waved the ancient envelope. "There's even a cutting from a newspaper describing the public hanging. It was a great scandal in its day and never mentioned again in our family. Poor Francis, he never fitted in; he needed money and never had enough. He grew up in a stately home and became a gambler. The women he loved refused to marry him, his family disowned him; the more his brother prospered, the lower he sank. It was as though one was born with all the virtues and the other with all the vices. But he was a superb horseman, by far the better of the two."

"So he *was* hung, then," said Carl, looking at me.

"Penniless and disowned. News travelled slowly, if at

all, in those days," said Dad. "And your great-great-grand-father wasn't the only coachman he killed. The news of his shameful death may never have reached your family."

Carl held out his hand and shook mine. It was a firm, steady handshake. "Our great-great-grandfather was a bit of a rogue too," he admitted. "They say he beat his wife and drove sick, lame and blind horses. You can't sink much lower than that, can you?"

"It was a different world," said Dad.

"I hope you will come and ride with us again soon, Francis," Melanie said, with an apologetic smile.

"And let bygones be bygones," added Carl.

The rain had stopped. When we opened the front door everything outside looked washed clean.

"I *do* believe in ghosts now," I said.

"I think we are nicer than our ancestors—much, much nicer," said Melanie to Dad. "I mean, a doctor is a far better person than a highwayman, isn't he."

"Why *did* you call me Francis, rather than James?" I asked after the Nelsons had left.

"I think because James was awful, too, but in a different way. He had everything, but he cheated and seduced young girls and rode horses to death in the hunting field. He was a hypocrite. He looked all right on the outside, but really his behaviour was appalling. At least Francis never pretended to be good . . ." explained Dad. "But perhaps we should have played safe and called you John," he added, laughing.

"I thought it was nice to have a ghost. Now I'm not so sure," I said.

"Your mother's family was O.K. They were the salt of the earth. Now . . . I must be off. I'm late," said Dad. "And, while I remember, don't ever again go riding at night without a light—or there'll be another ghost in the family!"

THE GHOSTLY GARDENERS

by RUTH CAMERON

RAIN was drizzling down. Flatly, patteringly. He accepted it as fitting for today's general awfulness. Funny how sometimes the weather corresponded with one's mood. His mood this evening was wet and grey. School had been diabolical. He'd felt unwell, yet had tried to keep up. The result? At P.E. he'd made his usual flying leap over the "horse"—and landed with a plonk on the middle of its back. Everyone had laughed, including the teacher. He'd hated them all and wanted to die.

How did one die anyway? What *was* death? Was it just an escape, a nothingness, a refuge, like a sleep without dreams? Or did one have to go on in some after-life, which might be even worse than this one? Who was to know? Certainly not the headmaster, who read out religious bits every morning in a sanctimonious voice. He obviously knew nothing about anything. He even whacked you on your bottom with a slipper if you broke a rule. What a way to carry on!

And the rain drizzled down, soaking the shoulders of his jacket, seeping in between the soles and tops of his shoes, so that he plodded in sludgy socks. He walked now alongside the high wall, which went on for a long time and gave one an oppressed feeling, as it made the pavement seem narrower and the swishing traffic in the roadway more violent and threatening.

He drew closer to this long, blank wall, as if it might offer him protection.

And he saw the door.

What an extraordinary thing! He had walked past this wall hundreds of times, in all sorts of weather and states

94

of mind, and he had never noticed that door before. Yet it was quite a noticeable door. For it was black.

If you think about it, there aren't that many black doors around.

Why had he never noticed it before?

Was it new?

He stood in the rain, which he had forgotten for the moment, and studied the black door.

No, it wasn't new. It looked pretty ancient. He saw a keyhole, but no handle. Unhopefully, he gave it a little push.

And it opened.

For a second, he shrank back, fearing, like any child, a cry from some indignant adult: "Who are you? What are you doing here? Scarper!"

But there was no sound. The door stayed wide open, and, inside, he saw green: green grass—green trees—green leaves—and even the grey sky seemed to be of a sort of greeny-yellow shade. It was a different world. And wasn't that just what he'd been wanting—a different world?

He went in. He left the black door open behind him and moved cautiously, timid as an animal on alien territory. He tiptoed.

His steps made no sound on the grass-green path which snaked across the vivid lawn. He could have taken short-cuts, but he didn't. He snaked with the path. After walking windingly for some time, he came to a black-and-green building.

It was as windowed as a greenhouse, but he couldn't see through the glass, which merely reflected the greenness of the surroundings. Also, the glass was blurred with rain. Not that he could feel any wetness now. He was too absorbed with curiosity to have any physical feelings. He was all mind.

He found the door of the black-and-green glasshouse, with its invisible interior, and turned the handle. It opened. He peered round.

Before him was one of the strangest sights he had ever seen.

The place *was* a kind of greenhouse, but the plants were such as he had never imagined. They were potted plants, but not the ordinary stuff you see in shop-windows. There were some which looked like miniature willow trees . . . some with stems which twisted like bent wire and had round, petal-less flowers on top . . . some which grew like upside-down arrows . . . some which looked like little human figures. And there was no colour anywhere, except the green, and the black, if you can call black a colour.

Three gardeners—or so he supposed them—moved about in this black-and-green-greenhouse. He could not see their faces, for hoods obscured their features; and they wore long black robes, like monks' habits, which made them figureless. Except that he could tell they were all thin. He was filled with wonder, and, strangely, was unafraid. For there was a gentleness in the movements of the black-robed figures as they tended their plants which made him feel that they would never hurt anyone. They only wanted things to grow.

One of them held a big, black watering-can and was sprinkling with water a tiny little black plant shaped like a six-pointed star. It was turning its minute face up to the water, drinking it in. The spray of water was clearest silver. Silver droplets gleamed on black petals.

Enchanted, he gazed.

Another of the gardeners moved over to a desk and began to write, as if he were a doctor, writing up a record of this plant "patient" or that. As he bent over his writing, his face was completely obscured by his big, black hood.

The third gardener was doing something at the far side of the green house. Only his back could be seen: thin, with broad shoulders, and the dark robe flowing off them like an ebony waterfall.

The three took no notice whatsoever of the intruder. It was as if he didn't exist. Well—they must have seen him, so, if they didn't object to his presence, he might as well have a good look around . . .

And he did.

He walked among the strange, potted plants arrayed on the shelves and examined each one, marvelling at the exotic shapes, the uniqueness of each cluster of leaves and petals, the mystery of it all.

He wished he could help to look after the plants. Was there maybe some little job he could do to assist the black-robed gardeners?

Which one dared he approach?

The one with the watering-can? He was watering another plant now—one of the baby weeping-willows. And as he did so, tears seemed to be dropping from under the hood he wore—tears as silver as the water from the can. But was it ordinary water? Or was it—well, what?—distilled moonlight?

He went right up to the figure with the watering-can.

"Excuse me," he said.

The head turned slightly in his direction, but still he could not see the face.

"Can I do anything to help?" he asked.

The hooded head gave a small shake, resigned rather than impatient. Oh, well, there seemed to be only one watering-can anyway. He looked across to the figure which had its back to him and saw the gardener's hands training some black creepers around a stick. And those hands paralysed him with sudden shock—for the fingers had no flesh on them. They were all bone. The hands then withdrew under the wide sleeves of the robe, and he wondered for a second if he'd imagined what he'd seen. Maybe the hands had merely been very thin, and the greenish light had given an illusion of fleshlessness.

Tentatively he moved towards the desk where the other figure was writing. Only the tips of the fingers showed. They were fleshless. That was no illusion. Who were these people? Lepers? Terribly sick men in some sort of hospital, and their gardening was a therapy? Fear was in him,

97

yet it still wasn't strong because of the seeming gentleness of the creatures, and the utter quietness.

"What is this place? Who are you?" he asked. His voice sounded overloud, crude and intrusive. "Sorry. I didn't mean to shout," he said quickly, "but please don't ignore me any more. Please tell me who you are. Look at me, anyway!"

The figure at the desk looked up at him. The one with the watering-can looked down at him. The one on the other side of the place looked across at him. With their fleshless hands, they pushed aside the folds of their hoods.

Three sad-expressioned skulls regarded him.

A black curtain, like a great black hood descended upon him and there was nothing but spinning darkness . . .

"I think he's coming round. Hello, lad. You all right?"

He was lying on the wet pavement alongside the high wall. Two men were bending over him. One of them helped him to his feet. "What happened, then? Did you fall over and knock your head?"

"No. I—I don't remember falling . . . Oh, yes, I did, though—a black thing came over me—they must have put a hood on me and carried me out here . . . Where are they? Where's the black door?"

"What black door?" asked the other man.

"In the wall. It was here. I went in——"

"You've been dreaming, son," said the first man. "There's no door in this wall."

"That's right," agreed his companion. "Never been no door in this wall, not never."

"I'd never noticed it until today," the boy explained. "It must have been new. Except that it was old."

The two men exchanged glances. "You're not quite yourself, son. Where do you live?" asked one of them. He told them, and the man said: "That's not far from me. I'll see you safely back. At least it's stopped raining now."

So the kind stranger saw him home and told his mother:

The figure at the desk looked up at him ...

"Your boy had a bit of a turn in the street, missus, but he seems to be all right now."

His mother was worried and, after the man had departed, asked: "What happened? What did he mean by a 'bit of a turn'?"

"I don't know, Mum. I just sort of passed out. I've been feeling grotty all day."

During the walk back he had decided not to say a word about the greenhouse and the three robed skeletons. He couldn't get their sad skulls and fleshless fingers out of his mind's eye. The plants haunted him, too. The whole scene had stayed alive within him, yet common sense told him that none of it could really have happened. There had been no black door. He had passed out and had a dream.

Yet it had been so real!

"Straight to bed with you," said his mother. "People don't faint in the street for no reason." And she sent for the doctor, who declared that the flu bug had got him and that there was a lot of it around. He spent a restless night, tangled with nightmares of grinning skulls and weird vegetation, and in the morning his mother said he must spend the day in bed. He wasn't sorry to do so. He felt weak and strange.

In the afternoon, when she brought him a cup of tea, he asked her: "Mum, what's on the other side of that long wall? You know—the one I walk past on my way back from school."

"It's the back wall of St. Dominic's, of course," she said. "Didn't you know? You've seen the front often enough."

It was true. He had. The front of St. Dominic's, now a college for training teachers, was in a different street altogether. Somehow he had never connected those prim premises with the long, mysterious, high wall. A nightmare thought came to him: Who trained teachers? Black-robed skeletons? Was that why teachers were so diabolical . . . ? No, no, no . . . What had happened to him had not happened . . . It couldn't have . . . He must hang on to that.

But it had happened. Even if it hadn't, it had. One day, when he was better, he must get into the grounds behind that college and find out what was there.

A week later, he was back at school, the flu bug conquered. He gave the high wall every chance first: he walked alongside it, looking for the door. No door. Right. Then he must enter by going round to the front. He'd be late home, but he could make some excuse—say he'd been "kept in".

He raced around the streets until he came to the front of the college. As he went in by the main entrance, he tried to look like a teacher-in-training. A dwarf teacher, maybe? He chuckled to himself. Then he remembered reading something written by a burglar, who had said: "Think yourself invisible. That's the trick. If you think yourself invisible, people won't see you."

Studiously thinking himself invisible, he walked up the front drive, then made his way across the grounds towards the back wall. He calculated where he was, where the greenhouse had been.

Now he was standing where the greenhouse should be. And there was no building there at all. But other things were the same—the greenness of everything, the trees, the grass, the leaves—and there was a sort of winding path, like the track of an invisible snake across the grass. That was the path he'd tiptoed along when he'd come through the black door.

But there was no black door, and no greenhouse.

It hadn't happened. It had all been a dream, because he was ill and had a fever . . . He must settle for that . . .

"Hello."

He nearly jumped out of his skin. He turned towards the voice, half-expecting to see a skeleton in a black robe . . .

Not at all. A most ordinary, middle-aged man stood there, looking like anyone's father.

"Hello," he said nervously. He was going to be ticked off now, for being here.

Instead, the man said lightly: "Do you know you're standing in a haunted spot?"

"No. Am I?"

"Indeed you are. Want to hear about it?"

"Please."

The man spread out his arms. "Long, long ago, there was a building here, where three Dominican monks performed miracles. They shouldn't have been here at all. No one knew they were. The old monastery had been sacked, and most of the Black Friars had fled—but these three stayed, secretly. They brewed herbs, made potions—and they had a secret back door, a black door, there——" He pointed to the blank wall. "People would come creeping through that door, to be healed by the three monks who weren't supposed to exist."

"If no one knew they were here, how did people know to come?"

"God knows," laughed the man. "Those who are sick, or falling sick, know where to come."

"I came," said the boy. "I met them. It was when I had flu."

"I remember," said the man. "Take my hand."

The boy held out his hand. The other took it. And, on the instant, the whole scene changed. They were in the greenhouse. The man who held his hand was black-robed, black-hooded, and, in his other hand, was holding a watering-can.

The formerly ordinary face looking down at him was no longer ordinary. It was a skull. Yet a gentle skull. It seemed to have a kindly expression. The hand which held his was that of a skeleton, quite fleshless—and yet he was not afraid.

"You were more ill than you knew," said the figure with the watering-can. "You were at Death's Door." He pointed. "See it?"

102

Yes, dimly through the glass of the greenhouse, he could see the black door in the wall.

"I left it open," the boy said, "when I came in before."

"Others have come in since and closed it behind them."

"What happened that other time? *Did* you fling something over my head and carry me outside?"

"Yes, but we gave you some medicine first, so that you'd recover quickly."

"A medicine made up from all these strange plants?"

"That's right. This is the Garden of Death. There are many such, all over the world. Only the sick see them. They come to us, and sometimes they stay, but most often we give them medicine and send them back, and nearly always they forget about us, or think that we were a dream. They forget us as a dream is forgotten."

"*I* thought you must be a dream."

"And you will think so again."

"Oh, no. This is so real." He looked at the figure at the desk, and the skull-face smiled at him; so did the more distant figure, tending climbing plants with his fleshless fingers.

"This explains," said the boy, "why some people get better quickly, even when they're very ill—miraculous cures and so forth. They're not 'miraculous' at all. You do it!"

The robed skeletons quivered with laughter, indeed, rattled a little as they chuckled. "That puts us in our places," said the one at the desk. "Not 'miraculous' at all —only us doing it."

"We thought you ought to know that the dead help the living, that we're not just a load of idle layabouts," said the one with the watering-can.

"But don't talk about it when you go back," said the one at the desk. "You won't be believed."

"I know that already," said the boy. "Don't worry. I won't give you away. Now—how do I get back?"

"Take my hand again," said the one with the watering-can.

As the boy did so, he found the fingers had become

covered with flesh again, the skull-face had become the fleshed face of the man he had met in the grounds, and the black robes had changed into an ordinary suit. The greenhouse and the black door had gone. "Go out by the front, the way you came," said the man.

"Who *are* you?"

"The Gardener. Go along, off with you. Don't speak of us, but remember us. Next time you need us, you'll find us without seeking us. Each time you come, we'll help to cure your sickness, and when at last you stay, you will join us in our work and help those who have been left behind. Goodbye for the present."

"Goodbye. Thank you." He walked away for a few yards, then looked back. The man had vanished, yet there was nowhere to vanish to.

A voice behind him said: "Looking for someone, lad?"

He turned. A man, casually dressed in shirt and rough trousers, stood there. "I was looking for that—that person I was talking to."

"Well, I've been standing watching you for some time, and you were talking to yourself," said the man. "I'm the gardener here, and don't you come wandering round again."

"You're not the real Gardener," said the boy. "In this garden, there is another garden, and a greenhouse with——" He stopped. *Don't speak of us, but remember us.* The voice came through the sound of the wind in the trees.

"I'm sorry," he murmured to the voice.

"That's all right," said the man, thinking the apology was meant for him. "You don't look too well, actually."

"I've only just got over flu."

"Ah, well, they fill you up with funny drugs nowadays to get you better, then you can get nasty side-effects. My wife went on a 'trip' after some antibiotic stuff she took. Go along home, and no more trespassing on private grounds."

As the boy moved away, the gardener said: "Did *you*

leave that thing there?" He pointed to the spot where the boy had been standing—the place where the greenhouse was invisible. What was not invisible, however, was the large black watering-can which stood proudly on the grass.

"It's not mine," said the boy. The gardener walked over to it. Sunshine suddenly looked down through the clouds. The man's shadow was clear on the grass. But the watering-can cast no shadow. And when the gardener bent to pick it up, he grasped at nothingness, and the "thing" vanished. The boy burst out laughing and ran away, still laughing. He glanced behind once, to see the gardener standing there, staring in utter wonder at the nothingness on the grass.

And the wind in the trees chuckled like a rattle of friendly bones, and the boy ran all the way home, laughing in the sunshine, for the ghostly gardeners had done the one thing that would make him believe in them for ever, and never fear them again: they had done something funny. They had played such a lovely joke!

THE OLD SIEGE HOUSE

by Sydney J. Bounds

"TALKING rabbits!" Cousin Alf jeered. "Why don't you grow up, Em?"

Alf was fourteen, big and beefy, and the smirk on his red face reminded Emma Watson of a cat playing with a mouse. She was two years younger and a lot smaller than her cousin.

They were following the course of a small stream that wound across the meadow when, suddenly, Alf snatched the copy of "Watership Down" from under Emma's arm.

"Give it back to me. And stop calling me Em—my name's Emma."

She tried to get the book back but it slipped between their hands and fell in the stream. She stood, sad-eyed, watching her favourite book float away out of reach.

"You're just a bully," she said, her voice trembling. But she wasn't going to let him see her cry. Not again. She knew he was just waiting to sneer, 'Cry baby!' That was his idea of fun.

Alf gave a horsy laugh. "Now I suppose you'll run home and tell Mummy. You do, and I'll pay you back. It was an accident, see?"

Emma knew it would be no good complaining. Cousin Alf had been ill, and her mother wasn't going to listen to any more grumbles about his behaviour.

She had guessed, with a sinking heart, what it would be like when Alf came to convalesce at Rosemary Cottage. Unfortunately she had been only too right; in a couple of weeks, her life had become a misery.

The telly never seemed to have anything on except cricket and horse-racing, and she missed all her favourite programmes. He was lazy and always demanding: "How about a cuppa for the invalid, then?"

It might have been different if Dad had been home, but he was away in Norway on business. And Mum was always busy, of course. To be fair to her, though, Alf rarely tried anything on when she was around.

Now his grating voice shouted at her. "C'mon, I want my tea. Are you going to stand there all day moaning over your silly book?"

Slowly Emma left the stream and followed him across the meadow. The summer sun was hot, and bees hummed through the air, alighting on flowers. Cows grazed quietly in the distance. Long grass, sprinkled with buttercups, swished about her legs. The path led around a small hill towards the village.

Presently Alf paused to let her catch up. He pointed to the top of the hill. "What's that up there?"

Emma and her parents had only recently moved into the country. "I'm not sure. I've heard it called Siege House."

"Looks like ruins," Alf said in an excited voice. "Let's explore."

Emma climbed after him up the hillside. The old house on the crest had once been big and proud, dominating the land for miles around. Now the grounds were overgrown with weeds, and the house appeared to be in a state of near-collapse. The half-timbered walls were split, one side sagging at an angle. Sections of the roof had fallen in, leaving gables and chimneys sticking up like part of the set of a Gothic film.

Alf scrambled over a pile of rubble to get inside.

"Is it safe?" Emma asked doubtfully.

"Safe?" His raucous voice filled with scorn. " 'Course it's safe. Hundreds of years old, I bet, and they built things to last then. It's still standing, ain't it? So it ain't going to fall down now."

Emma climbed carefully over the rubble and followed him through a rotting doorway into the house. There was a wide hall with doors opening off it, and stairs that went up to the open sky. The floor was thick with dust, and Emma saw Alf's footprints clearly as he went exploring; there were no other prints at all. The windows that remained were dark and grimy, and the huge open chimney was piled high with soot.

Despite the heat of the sun overhead, Emma shivered. There was something oppressive about the silence. She thought there ought to be the creaking of ancient timbers, or the scurrying of mice. Instead, there was nothing. The silence was absolute . . .

Not quite. Emma heard the sound of heavy breathing near her, a voice that whispered, and another, fainter, answering.

Alf was across the hall, peering through a doorway into another room. It was only an echo, she told herself.

"What did you say?" she called.

"Me? I didn't say nothing."

From the corner of her eye, Emma thought she saw something move. It was just a blur. She turned quickly, but there was no one there. She stared at a blank brick wall and shivered.

Alf sauntered across the dusty hall. "Smashing place, this. We'll come back and explore properly later. Perhaps there's cellars we can . . . What's up now?"

Emma gave a startled cry and nearly jumped out of her skin as an icy hand touched her shoulder from behind. Alf was in front of her, five yards away, staring at her. She whirled round but, of course, there was nobody else in the room.

Or was there? For a moment, eyes straining to see into a shadowy corner, she glimpsed thin, pale faces.

"So many of them!" she cried out.

And from somewhere far off came the clash of metal on metal.

"You must have heard that, Alf."

"So what?" he grunted. "It's only the wind. Always knew there was something wrong with you—Come on, I'm hungry."

Emma wasn't sorry to leave the ruined house and hurried after her cousin as he climbed over the rubble. Outside, the sun was hot and there was no wind. She glanced back.

The house stood solitary among the weeds and brambles, silent, and obviously deserted. It was just an old ruin and nothing more. Why, then, did a chill run along her spine? As they walked home together, she decided it was not a place she wanted to visit ever again.

Next morning, her mother said: "I'd like you to go into town and do some shopping for me." She smiled. "It'll give you a rest from Alfred."

With a basket and shopping list, Emma took the hourly bus into Dale. It did not take long to complete the shopping and, while she waited for the bus back, she browsed among the racks outside a secondhand bookshop.

She was surprised to find a slim booklet with, on the cover, a picture of the house on the hill. The title read:

LOCAL HISTORY SERIES
No. 4: The Old Siege House

As the booklet had been reduced in price to just a few pence, Emma bought it out of curiosity.

Back at Rosemary Cottage, peace didn't last long. After lunch, Alf said: "C'mon, Em, I'm bored, so we'll play football."

He trotted out into the garden, bouncing his ball. Emma sighed and followed reluctantly. He kicked the ball hard at her, and she dodged.

"Not like that! You're supposed to kick it back. Now, dribble it—see if you can get past me. Bet you can't!"

Nervously Emma obeyed, and Alf charged like an excited bull. His shoulder hit her and knocked her down, and he kicked the ball away. Breathless, Emma picked herself up and limped towards the house.

"Sissy!" he shouted.

Emma's mother appeared in the doorway. "That's quite enough of that, Alfred."

Indoors, Emma reached for the booklet she had bought that morning and curled up with it in a chair by the window. Inside, she was surprised to see a line drawing of a castle, standing on a hill and surrounded by a moat. She began to read:

The Old Siege House, as it is called today, was originally a manor house built on the site of Rothsay Castle. It is the castle that has the more interesting history, and the present name dates from a later period. It does not appear to have been called Siege House until after the first reports of the haunting. From that time, the house has not been lived in and has gradually fallen into disrepair. The local people are reluctant to enter its grounds even now.

The castle was adulterine: that is to say, a castle built in Stephen's reign without royal permission. It stood until the time of Henry III. When, in 1224, the King demanded that it be handed over to the crown, the Earl of Rothsay defied the royal forces to take the castle, and the siege began. It lasted from June 22nd until August 15th. Starvation weakened the defenders and, when the castle was finally stormed, the rebels were put to death without mercy

Five days after this, the demolition of the castle began. The moat was filled in, and the stones sent away to churches and priories, so that never again could the castle be used as a stronghold by powerful barons usurping the King's powers. Today it is impossible to trace the shape of that formidable castle.

Legend states that it is the storming of the castle that has left its ghostly residue . . .

"What's this?" Alf demanded suddenly. "Another of your silly books?"

He had crept up silently and snatched the booklet out of Emma's hand. He read aloud in a mocking voice:

"On each anniversary, the ghostly siege is re-enacted . . . The stuff you read, Em! Ghosts, now. August the fifteenth —that's next week. All right, we'll go back there on the fifteenth and I'll show you there's no such thing as ghosts!"

When the morning of the anniversary came, the sun

shone from a cloudless sky. Alf, on his best behaviour, had no trouble persuading Emma's mother to provide a picnic lunch. They set off down the lane, Emma carrying the haversack.

Alf set a brisk pace, leaving the lane and crossing the meadow directly towards the house on the hill. Emma looked up at the ruins and her heart sank. Despite the sunny day, there was nobody else in sight; it really did look as if the villagers avoided the place.

"Perhaps this isn't such a good idea," she said, lagging behind.

"I'm not letting you back out now," Alf said. "You're the one who believes this rubbish, not me." He dragged her up the hillside.

"You're hurting me," Emma complained.

"Just remember, *I* can hurt you—a ghost can't."

In blazing sunlight, they climbed the hill towards the ruins on the crest.

"Pity there's nothing left to see of the castle," Alf said. "Now that would have been interesting."

He helped Emma over the rubble and into Siege House. Out of the sun, the air struck chill. It was as if a dark cloud passed between the house and the sky; even Alf noticed a difference, and shivered.

Emma stood in the centre of the big hall, watching Alf's footprints in the dust as he raced around, shouting: "Bring out your ghosts! I'm waiting!"

His laughter echoed about the ruins, and the echoes faded into silence. The silence had a dead quality, as though a damp blanket hung in the air. Then Emma heard other sounds, faint at first, but steadily gaining in volume: confused shouting and shrill cries, followed by the blast of a horn.

Alf came to a sudden halt. "What's that?"

Startled, Emma looked through a gap in the wall. Outside, men in chain mail and carrying pikes charged up the hillside. She gasped as some of them dropped when a flight of arrows struck home.

She saw that she was surrounded by pale, thin figures with gaunt faces; they were all about her in the hall. Hall? She saw stone walls with arrow loops.

"What's happening?" Alf's voice was suddenly scared. "Where are we?"

The layer of dust had vanished; the stone floor was covered by rushes. Emma's nose wrinkled at the smell of unwashed bodies.

She trembled, and her voice came out shaky. "Do you see them, too?"

Alf's face had gone chalk-white. Through the ghostly shouting, he mumbled: "I don't like this."

There came the pounding of a heavy wooden ram at the massive gateway. It burst inward and armed men poured through, yelling and brandishing swords. Metal clashed against metal as desperate men hacked and clubbed at each other. The air rang with cries of hate and despair.

His teeth rattling like castanets, Alf backed away. His eyes glazed with fear, and his mouth opened and made meaningless croaking noises.

Emma saw the madness of battle-crazed faces and heard the shrieks of the dying. She watched in horror as a bloodied pike lunged right through her cousin to reach one of the defenders.

The haunting was too much for Alf. Terrified, he turned tail and ran, screaming . . .

His action released Emma from the paralysis that had gripped her. Clutching the haversack with their picnic lunch, she ran through the phantom mêlée after him. Out in the sun again, she looked back at an empty and silent ruin.

She slowed to a walk and, by the time she reached home, her heart had stopped its violent throbbing.

Her mother came swiftly towards her. "What on earth has happened to Alfred? He's as white as a sheet, and I can't get a word out of him."

"We went to Siege House, and Mum——" Emma's

words came with a rush—"It really is haunted and I'll never go back there again."

Emma's mother studied her in silence, then she said briskly: "I think that's a very sensible decision, Emma. Now, why don't you both have your picnic in the garden?"

After they had finished the sandwiches and sausage rolls and lemonade, Alf's colour came back. So did his loud and bullying voice.

"O.K., Em, I'll tell you what—we'll do a spot of tree-climbing."

"You can," Emma said quietly. "I don't feel like it."

Alf clenched his right hand and raised it menacingly. "You have to do what I want," he blustered.

Emma laughed. "Not any more, Cousin Alf. You forget—I've seen just how big and brave you really are. About as big and brave as a rather small mouse, I should say."

Alf stared at her, then slowly lowered his fist and looked away.

THE HOUSE GHOSTS

by MARY DANBY

THE street was grey with December rain as the postman stopped outside Number 19 and took from the bundle of letters in his hand a pale mauve envelope addressed to Mrs. Wetherby. He glanced about him, then furtively held it to his nose for a moment before slipping it through the letter-box. His face, as he turned away, showed clearly that he, for one, was happy not to be on the receiving end of a violet-scented letter.

In the hall of Number 19, Mrs. Wetherby picked up the letter—a little gingerly, on account of the smell—and began to read it. Her eyes widened with dismay. "Oh, no!" she groaned. "How simply ghastly!"

Her daughter Wendy, on her way through to the kitchen, paused. "What's up?"

"It's from Aunt Prudence," said Mrs. Wetherby. "Your grandmother's cousin, remember? She came for a weekend once and you said you hoped she'd never come again. Well . . ."

"Yes . . . ?" said Wendy suspiciously.

"Aunt Prudence usually goes to Bournemouth for Christmas, to stay with her sister Mildred. *She's* pretty dreadful, too—all luncheon meat and dog hairs. We used to call her Aunt Mouldy. Anyway, it seems Aunt Prudence needs a break from her. 'There's a train arriving around four o'clock on December 23rd,' she says, 'and no doubt I can find a taxi to bring me from the station. How nice that we shall all be together for Christmas.' "

Wendy stood quite still, drinking in the horror of it all. Then she said: "Must we? I mean, do we really have to? Couldn't you write back and say we've all got chicken-pox?"

114

"It's a bit late for that," Mrs. Wetherby said miserably. "She's arriving the day after tomorrow."

"But it's Christmas," Wendy complained. "We *can't* have her here for Christmas. She'll ruin everything. You know how putrid she is. She's a monster. Five-star."

Aunt Prudence was one of those people who arrived and took over. Everything had to be organized her way—which was usually nobody else's way, and anyone daring to voice an opinion she didn't agree with was dealt a withering look and punished in some subtly infuriating way, such as being sent to turn the house upside-down for Aunt Prudence's reading glasses, when all the time they were right next to her, in her handbag. ("Well, fancy that, now!") If the gas fire was on, Aunt Prudence chose the heat setting. When the daily newspaper arrived, Aunt Prudence would collar it—and read it maddeningly slowly. At mealtimes, she always took the first of everything, and the last. She was indeed monstrous.

"I suppose we'll have to buy her some sort of Christmas present," said Mrs. Wetherby, sighing heavily.

"A boa constrictor?" suggested Wendy.

The news of Aunt Prudence's visit filled the house with gloom. The lights on the Christmas tree seemed to dim to half their brightness, and the decorations sagged mournfully. Mr. Wetherby sat for a long while, staring into space, while the two boys, Peter and Danny, wandered aimlessly from room to room, egging each other on in their disgust at the situation.

"Think of her voice," said Danny. "It's like a rusty chain saw."

"She's a pig. Prudence Pig. Fat, greedy and revoltingly pink," said Peter.

"Yuk!" said Danny. "And she smells like carnations. Dead ones."

"She goes on and on. On and on and on, she goes. On and on."

"She always bags the best chair."

"The biggest cake."

115

"The crispiest potato."

"I wish she'd go to Timbuctoo," said Peter.

"Blinkistan," said Danny.

"Where's that?" said Peter.

"Nowhere. I made it up."

By the evening, however, they had more or less resigned themselves to the Coming of Aunt Prudence. "We'll pretend she's not there." But this was something of an optimistic idea, and it was a far from cheerful family which finally went upstairs to bed.

Later on, when the only remaining light came from the street-lamps outside, two shadowy figures gradually appeared in the armchairs on either side of the hearth. One was an elderly gentleman in a velvet smoking jacket, the other, a short, stoutish woman who wore a straight, ankle-length skirt topped by a lacy blouse, a long, jet necklace and a rather attractive maroon shawl she had crocheted herself. Albert and Victoria were brother and sister. About fifty years before the Wetherby family had bought Number 19, Albert and Victoria had lived there. Died there, in fact. And now they returned to it from time to time, as they had quite a fondness for the old grey building. "House Ghosts," they were known as, in the Order of Beyond.

Number 19 was strong and solid, made to last, with tall sash windows on either side of the glazed porch. In the days when Albert and Victoria lived there, a maid had scrubbed the steps once a week. Now the steps were dark and dingy, but the house was bright within, and the brother and sister were glad to hear it ring with laughter and the shouts of children.

"Such a shame," said Victoria, tidying a strand of her silver hair into the bun at the nape of her neck. "They always have such a jolly Christmas, and now that appalling Aunt Prudence is going to spoil it all. I remember when she came here before. She ate all the chocolate biscuits at tea."

"Reminds me of Great Aunt Isobel," said Albert. "Now, she was almost worse, wasn't she. Never used to allow any

116

fun at all. She said the noise of merrymaking was like the bells of Hell calling us to damnation." He shuddered. "I can see her now. Like a pencil, she was—tall and straight and grey." His moustache quivered at the memory.

"The thing is," said Victoria, "what are we going to do about the dreaded Aunt Prudence?"

"Do?" queried Albert. "I don't see what we *can* do. If she's coming, she's coming."

Victoria gave a hopeful little smile. "But, couldn't we ... couldn't we make things just a bit ... how can I put it ... *disturbing* for her?"

"Are you saying what I think you're saying?" Albert asked, frowning.

"Just this once ... ?"

Albert shook his head. "Out of the question, my dear. You know it's against the rules. We're allowed to visit, but we mustn't haunt. Otherwise we might be exorcised, and we wouldn't want that to happen. Remember Percy Blick."

Percy Blick had been a friend of theirs, a one-time Town Councillor, now a Dear Departed, who had taken to floating wispily through the middle of council meetings and blowing cold air at the back of the mayor's neck every time he didn't like what was being discussed. Eventually, a priest had been called to get rid of him. Some words were said in Latin, and the priest sprinkled holy water here and there, and the next thing Albert and Victoria heard was that Percy had his Visitor's Pass taken away and had been banished to the Great Void for a year and a day.

"Remember Percy Blick," Albert repeated. "We wouldn't want that to happen to us. No—spectral appearances, moans, rattling chains ... I'm afraid we couldn't risk it."

Victoria thought for a while. "Suppose we didn't actually *appear*," she said slowly. "Suppose there just happened to be one or two little accidents ... Nothing that would make them suspect us, of course. But Aunt Prudence might find her stay the teeniest bit uncomfortable, don't you think?" She looked hopefully at her brother, who was sucking gently at his teeth as he considered the matter. "I mean, we can't just sit here and do nothing at all," she concluded.

"Hm . . . hm . . . Very well, then," Albert said eventually, "as it is in such a good cause. But we must take care not to let them think they are being haunted. Of course," he added, "I wouldn't even consider it, but for the memory of Christmas 1883, ruined so disastrously by the cheerless presence of Great Aunt Isobel. No, Aunt Prudence must be seen to."

"Oh—spiffing!" said Victoria.

On the day before Christmas Eve, at about four-thirty in the afternoon, Aunt Prudence arrived. She wore a huge pink mohair coat, which made her look even more bulky than ever, and perched on her lilac-rinsed curls was a red pillbox hat, so that she could have been mistaken, at a distance, for a pink blancmange with a cherry on the top.

"Aunt Prudence. How nice," said Mrs. Wetherby, opening the door wide so that the pink blancmange could wobble into the hall. "Children!" she called. "Aunt Prudence is here. Come down and say hello." There was no sound. "At once!" she demanded.

Wendy appeared at the top of the stairs, and at that moment there was a violent crash as the front door apparently slammed itself shut. The noise was so loud that Aunt Prudence jumped sideways, and her little red hat slid down to her nose just as a paper-chain came unstuck from the ceiling and descended over her shoulders.

"Must have been the wind," said a surprised-looking Mrs. Wetherby.

"Hello, Aunt Prudence," said Wendy, smothering a smile as she walked down the stairs. "How Christmassy you look."

"Don't smirk, girl. It doesn't become you," said Aunt Prudence, readjusting her hat and removing the paper-chain. "Yes, you're too thin, I remember that. It's ugly to be so thin. Is tea ready, Helen? I'm famished."

Mrs. Wetherby led the way into the sitting-room and brought in a tray of tea and cakes. Danny and Peter at last came down to say a reluctant hello.

"One cake each," said their mother.

As the two boys reached towards the plate, Aunt Prudence said smugly: "Visitors first," and stretched out a hand for the biggest and best—a large slice of chocolate cream gateau. But as she lifted it towards the gaping cavern of her mouth it somehow managed to slip out of her hand and land a squidgy mess on her lap.

"What a horrible, clumsy little boy," Aunt Prudence said to Peter, waving a pink, piggy finger at him. "You jogged my elbow."

Peter shook his head and looked toward his mother. "I didn't. Honestly, I didn't. I wasn't even anywhere near."

Aunt Prudence turned to Danny. "Fetch a damp cloth," she demanded. "Damp, mind, not wet. And while you're doing that, I'll have the cake that would have been Peter's. Perhaps it will teach him not to answer back, eh?" She stretched her rosebud mouth into a smug smile. "This one, I think . . . " Mrs. Wetherby protested, but Aunt Prudence pretended not to hear. "I do like a nice éclair," she said. "What a shame there's only the one."

Later, when Mr. Wetherby came home, the whole family settled down to watch the television. Aunt Prudence had brought her knitting—a large, shapeless splodge of turquoise and apricot, which, she said, was on its way to becoming a bedjacket. While she knitted, the balls of wool would keep slipping from her lap to the floor. No matter how securely she lodged them, they managed to roll off, and she tut-tutted to herself and made one of the children pick them up again. By the eighth time, she was getting very rattled indeed, but Danny and Peter were enjoying it all hugely, holding out their hands to catch the wool before it reached the floor.

Just then, the clock in the hall struck seven.

"Oh good, time for my programme," announced Aunt Prudence.

Mr. and Mrs. Wetherby looked at each other.

"But we're watching this film," said Wendy. "There's still half an hour to go."

"I always watch my programme," Aunt Prudence persisted. "Kindly switch over to the other channel."

Wendy turned to her father for help, but he just shrugged his shoulders, as if to say: "What's the use of fighting it? We might as well grit our teeth and suffer in silence."

Aunt Prudence's programme turned out to be *The Oldies*—a long-running serial about life in an old people's home, which made her chortle and cluck and shake her head from side to side, while the Wetherby family sat about in various attitudes of boredom, wishing they could turn back to *Duel in the Dust*. After *The Oldies* had been on for two or three minutes, however, the picture began to go round and round.

"Really!" said Aunt Prudence, pursing her lips. "Oh, do fix it, someone."

Mr. Wetherby fixed it. Then the colour faded to black and white. Mr. Wetherby fixed it. Then the screen became covered with little white spots. Then zig-zag lines appeared. Then the sound went alternately loud and soft.

"I don't think much of this television," complained Aunt Prudence. "The one I have at home is a great deal better."

"Well, go back to it, then," muttered Danny under his breath.

"Let's try the other channel," Wendy suggested hopefully. She pressed a button and, within seconds, all the faults vanished. "Looks as though we'd better watch the film after all," she said brightly.

"Hm," grunted Aunt Prudence. "It's never like this at Mildred's in Bournemouth. I dare say it's your Christmas tree lights. They use up all the electricity."

When everyone was in bed that night, and sound asleep, Albert and Victoria once more took shape before the cold hearth. In their day, it would have been the dying embers of a good coal fire in front of them—and a thick, smoky

120

fog outside. But Albert and Victoria didn't mind the absence of a fire; heat and cold had meant nothing to them for fifty years.

"Oh, isn't this good fun," Victoria said gaily. "Aunt Prudence is quite, quite dreadful, but I thought when you made her drop that cake I'd die laughing. Well, if I wasn't dead already, of course."

Albert chuckled. "What flummoxed me," he said, "was how you knew how to make that television go wrong. You never used to be much good with machines."

"Easy," said Victoria, smiling happily. "I just twiddled all the knobs in turn. They were too busy looking at the picture to notice what the knobs were doing."

Albert rose from his chair and walked thoughtfully around the room, stroking his moustache, then he took out his pocket watch, said "Ah!" and announced: "It's Christmas Eve, my dear. We have only a few hours left to achieve our purpose. Come, let's see if we can spoil someone's beauty sleep . . ."

Upstairs, Aunt Prudence lay wrapped in dreams, her lilac hair encased in a net and her mouth trembling slightly as she breathed out with little pop-pop-popping snores.

"The window," whispered Albert, gliding over to it and lifting the catch. In a moment, an icy wind was shifting the curtains and playing around the bed. Aunt Prudence moved sleepily and pulled the covers high over her neck.

Victoria, unseen at the foot of the bed, immediately gave a little tug, and the covers once more slipped down. With a grunt, Aunt Prudence pulled them up again. Up and down, up and down they went, while the room became colder and colder. A gentle twitch, to one side this time, and the eiderdown slid to the floor.

With a moan of annoyance, Aunt Prudence sat up and rubbed her eyes. Seeing the window open, she heaved herself out of bed and waddled over in her salmon-pink nightgown to close it. Then, muttering crossly, she climbed back into bed and heaved herself on to one side, hugging the bedclothes to her chin. Soon, she was once more snoring.

Aunt Prudence sat up . . .

"Right?" whispered Victoria.

"Right."

While Albert once more unlatched the window, Victoria slowly and carefully untucked the covers from the foot of the bed and rolled them back so that Aunt Prudence's fat pink toes would feel the full benefit of the wintry draught.

"Sweet dreams!" they whispered, and then they were gone.

In the morning, Mrs. Wetherby looked up from the stove as Aunt Prudence came into the kitchen. "Sleep well?" she asked brightly.

Aunt Prudence settled herself at the kitchen table. "I most certainly did not," she said. "That room has a faulty window catch, for a start, and the bedclothes are too small. My blankets were forever coming untucked. Then, this morning, I ran myself a hot bath—full to the brim, to warm myself up—but while I was fetching something from the bedroom, someone pulled out the plug. That Peter, if you ask me."

"Oh dear, what a shame," Mrs. Wetherby said sympathetically, turning towards the stove so that Aunt Prudence could not see her face. Serve the old bag right, she thought, for taking all the hot water. "Never mind," she went on. "Have some porridge—that should make you feel better." She began to ladle some porridge into a bowl, and at that moment Mr. Wetherby and the children came into the kitchen.

"Hurry up and sit down," said Mrs. Wetherby, turning away from the stove. "Porridge, everyone?"

Aunt Prudence glanced menacingly at Peter, then inspected the bowl which Mrs. Wetherby placed in front of her. "Porridge, is it?" she asked, prodding it with her spoon. She helped herself to milk and sugar and gave it all a good stir. Then, her eyes narrowing with greed, she raised the spoon to her mouth.

What happened next was so quick that no one was quite sure afterwards how it had all come about.

With a gurgling cry, Aunt Prudence pushed away her porridge bowl and jumped to her feet. Unfortunately, Danny's skateboard had somehow found its way under the table, and Aunt Prudence's feet, landing on it, shot forward, causing her to fall. As she fell, she clutched at the tablecloth, and so ended up slumped on the floor, drenched in orange juice and milk, with a pot of marmalade in her lap and a bowl of porridge upside down on her head.

. . . Of course, she wouldn't stay a moment longer. Definitely not. She was off to Mildred's in Bournemouth. There was still time to get a train, thank goodness. As Mr. Wetherby got the car out, ready to drive her to the station, the rest of the family gathered by the front door.

"Goodbye, Aunt Prudence," they said, one after the other. "We're so sorry . . ."

With a loud sniff, and a toss of her porridge-damp curls, she was gone, and the sound of the departing car was lost in the shouts of glee.

"Good riddance!" yelled Peter.

"Bad rubbish!" bellowed Danny.

"Merry Christmas!" said Wendy.

"Wasn't it odd," said Mrs. Wetherby, "how everything went wrong for her. She seemed to be haunted by bad luck."

"Not at all," Wendy replied. "She brought it all on herself."

Up in the spare bedroom, now mercifully free of Aunt Prudence's belongings, Albert and Victoria sat on the bed, laughing till the tears slid down their misty cheeks.

"All that pepper in her porridge . . ." chuckled Victoria. "And the skateboard—oh, the skateboard!"

"We did it," said Albert, leaning lazily back against the pillows. "We actually did it. And they didn't suspect a thing. Now we can all have a really jolly Christmas. I think perhaps we might join the family for their Christmas dinner . . . watch them pulling crackers, putting on their funny hats—not so's they'll notice us, of course," he added hurriedly.

Victoria had risen from the bed and was wandering about the room. "Albert," she said quietly, "look at the curtains . . ."

Although the window appeared to be firmly closed, the curtains were moving, as if stirred by a breeze. A strangely familiar chill seemed to rise from floor level.

Albert sat up. "What on earth . . . ?" he said.

There was a strong smell of wintergreen, and then a tall, slim form slowly took shape in the middle of the room. A long, dark grey dress, spectacles on a chain, a face as sharp and cold as a chisel.

"Oh m-m-my!" gasped Victoria.

"Hell's bells!" cursed Albert. "It's Great Aunt Isobel!"

The figure spoke. "Albert . . . Victoria . . ." it said, in a voice reminiscent of a chalk squealing across a blackboard, "how very nice to see you. I thought I would give you a pleasant surprise. I've come to stay—for Christmas."

ARMADA MONSTER BOOKS Nos. 1-4

Edited by R. Chetwynd-Hayes

Meet dozens of the most fearsome creatures ever to have menaced the earth – or slithered out of the sea – in three bumper collections of monster stories.

Monster's like Dimblebee's Dinosaur, frozen for centuries ... The Sad Vampire, who didn't like blood ... The terrible, three-headed Chimaera ... The awful underwater menace at Hell's Mouth ... The appalling Thing in the Pond ... The loathsome Lambton Worm ... The smiling Green Thing with the human head ... The dreaded, death-dealing Water Horse ... The Gargoyle that came knocking at the door ... and lots more mysterious, marvellous, murderous monsters.

How many Armada Spinechillers have you got?

Armada

Armada Science Fiction

Step into the strange world of Tomorrow with Armada's exciting science fiction series.

ARMADA SCI-FI 1
ARMADA SCI-FI 2
ARMADA SCI-FI 3
ARMADA SF 4

Edited by Richard Davis

Four spinechilling collections of thrilling tales of fantasy and adventure, specially written for Armada readers.

Read about . . . The monstrous Aliens at the bottom of the garden . . . A jungle planet inhabited by huge jellies . . . A robot with a human heart . . . The terrible, terrifying Trodes . . . A mad scientist and his captive space creatures . . . The deadly rainbow stones of Lapida . . . The last tyrannosaur on earth . . . and many more.

Stories to thrill you, stories to amuse you—and stories to give you those sneaking shivers of doubt . . .

Begin your sci-fi library soon!

Armada

has a whole shipload of exciting books for you

Armadas are chosen by children all over the world. They're designed to fit your pocket, and your pocket money too. They're colourful, gay, and there are hundreds of titles to choose from. Armada has something for everyone:

Mystery and adventure series to collect, with favourite characters and authors . . . like Alfred Hitchcock and The Three Investigators – the Hardy Boys – young detective Nancy Drew – the intrepid Lone Piners – Biggles – the rascally William – and others.

Hair-raising Spinechillers – Ghost, Monster and Science Fiction stories. Fascinating quiz and puzzle books. Exciting hobby books. Lots of hilarious fun books. Many famous stories. Thrilling pony adventures. Popular school stories – and many more.

You can build up your own Armada collection – and new Armadas are published every month, so look out for the latest additions to the Captain's cargo.

Armadas are available in bookshops and newsagents.

Armada